Caroline
and the
Tenderfoot

Manhunter Series, Book 3

Major Mitchell

majormitchell.net

Copyright © 2023 by Major Mitchell.

All rights reserved. No part of this book may be used or reproduced in any form whatsoever without written permission except in the case of brief quotations in critical articles or reviews.

This book is a work of fiction. Names, characters, businesses, organizations, places, events and incidents either are the product of the author's imagination or are used fictitiously.

http://www.majormitchell.net

Cover design by Karen Borrelli

ISBN-979-8-218-41240-1

Printed in the United States of America.

ALSO BY THIS AUTHOR

A Reason to Believe
The Valley of Decision
Poverty Flat
Canyon Wind

The Chase McGraw Series

Finding Grace
Jenny's Hope

The Doña Series

The Doña
Mokelumne Gold

The Manhunter Series

Manhunter
Where the Green Grass Grows

The Dusty Boots Series

Dusty Boots
Joker's Play
Refugio's Gold
Cool Water Justice

Caroline
and the
Tenderfoot

Chapter 1

April, 1898

The chugging of the engine became labored as black smoke bellowed from the smokestack. The train had hit a long incline and was struggling to get to the top. The small group of girls sitting two rows ahead of Thaddeus in one of the passenger cars had been talking non-stop since they boarded the train in Chicago. Thaddeus Jackson glared over the top of his newspaper, wishing for them by the mercy of God to be quiet, even for a few moments. He had never considered himself a violent man, but their constant chatter was causing him to imagine things that could happen to them that would give him a few moments of peace. There was one girl in particular sitting with her back toward him, who seemed to have a story or answer for every situation or question the others might have.

Several young men about the same age as the girls had boarded at the same time, but evidently were not part of the same group as he had first thought. They chose seats several rows away from the girls and were quietly reading. Thaddeus' fourteen-year-old sister, Beverly, sat in the seat facing him reading a ten-cent novel she had purchased at a Chicago bookstore. She had maybe spoken a couple of dozen words since they had boarded the train. He couldn't help but wonder why this group of girls couldn't be more like Beverly.

His father, Thaddeus Jackson the First, had surprised him by handing him train tickets from Chicago to El Dorado, Kansas. "Go buy a large herd of horses for us. With the feud between Spain and America, the U.S. could be drawn into a full-fledged war in a matter of months. If that happens, the military will want as many horses as they can lay their hands on." He paused to light his pipe.

"If we can find the horses and resell them to the government at a higher price, we'll make ourselves a tidy little sum."

"And what if that war never happens?"

"Then we'll sell our horses and recoup our cost. Either way we won't be out anything. And it's a whole lot better than watching you tinker on that horseless carriage in the barn."

His father reached into a drawer in his desk and handed Thaddeus a thick envelope.

"This should be enough to tide you and your sister over until you've found the horses."

"My sister?" Thaddeus had to fight to keep from laughing in the old man's face.

"Yes, Beverly only wanted one gift for her fourteenth birthday." Thaddeus Sr. drew deep on the pipe and released a cloud of smoke. "She wanted a trip out west, and I think this is a perfect way to give it to her. What's the matter? Do you disagree with your father?"

"No." Thaddeus drug the word out, not wanting to offend his father to his face. His dad was a big man who had arrived in America from Ireland with a twenty-dollar gold piece in his pocket and became extremely wealthy through hard work and a brilliant mind. There were only a few times Thaddeus could remember disagreeing with the old man's investments, only to discover his father saw something nobody else saw and pounced on the opportunity like a cat. But having to chaperone his fourteen-year-old sister on a business trip was going to be almost impossible. All she liked to do was lay around and read. He doubted he would find many horses inside a hotel room or library.

"Then, what's eating at you, son?"

"It's just that, how am I supposed to buy horses and take care of a fourteen-year-old girl at the same time? Besides, I honestly don't know much about horses, Dad, except for riding in a carriage being pulled by one every now and then."

"Yes, I know you'd rather ride in that noisy pile of scrap metal you have stored inside the barn.

Thaddeus cringed at the mention of the shiny red carriage tucked inside his father's horse barn. He'd always been curious about what was new. Even at a very young age, he'd rather take his toys apart to see how they worked than play with them.

He happened to be on hand when Charles and Frank Duryea put several of their autocars up for sale and Thaddeus bought one. After allowing a group of friends and family in Chicago to view the autocar and take rides, he promptly drove the vehicle to the barn and started dismantling it. When he finished assembling it again, the autocar had a fringed surrey top, a front lamp for night driving and two more lamps, one for each side of the vehicle. He had also extended the frame to hold a second seat to carry two extra passengers.

The autocar was powered by a four-horsepower internal combustion engine that Thaddeus believed would reach 10 miles per hour on a straight, level road. The problem was, places where a man could find a level road or buy fuel were few and far between.

"Besides," his father continued with a grin, "the average factory worker makes about $12.98 per week. You've got $1,000 invested in that bucket of bolts. Who can afford to buy one? No, it's a great hobby for you son, but not a living.

"I've taken the liberty to have one of the servants lay two books about horses on your bed and," he chuckled, "I have a feeling Beverly will end up taking care of you, instead of you taking care of her. Now, those tickets are for the day after tomorrow. Don't lose them."

******

Thaddeus glared at the headline in the newspaper he had brought from home. Georges Bouton and Charles Trépardoux had just won a race between autocars in France. It was being reported as a symbol of progress and innovation, and many were excited about this possibility for a new method of transportation.

He had left his father's office feeling like he'd been sentenced to exile. That should have been his image on the front page, not those other guys. He didn't know why his father wanted to invest money in horses for the military in the first place. He was far from being poverty-stricken. Quite the contrary. But to Thaddeus Jackson Sr., outwitting your opponent and making large sums of money was like a game of chess that he was very good at and Thaddeus Jackson Jr. had thought he wanted to be part of it. Now he wasn't so sure.

Thaddeus glanced at his sister whose chin was now resting on her chest. She had fallen asleep. He quietly slipped a bookmark between the opened pages of Beverly's book and gently closed it and sat back. With the constant chugging of the engine and the clack-clack-clacking of the tracks, Thaddeus himself dozed off and didn't wake until the train began to slow and the porter came through their car chanting, "Next stop, El Dorado, Kansas. Next stop, El Dorado, Kansas."

The landscape outside the passenger car window had suddenly changed. Thad could see what looked like two oil derricks with more oil derricks being built. Men and women were scurrying up and down the plank walkways. A man was escorted from a saloon and tossed into the muddy street as the slow-moving train passed. The town seemed to have its share of horseless carriages buzzing up and down the streets, coughing out small clouds of smoke. One larger vehicle loaded with drilling equipment was stuck in a big puddle of mud and the driver was cursing as he kicked one of the wooden spoked wheels.

Beverly blinked her eyes open and stretched with a yawn, then smiled at Thaddeus. "Oh, my. How long was I asleep?"

"I don't exactly know," Thaddeus said as he checked his pocket watch. "I fell asleep too, but I would venture to guess you were asleep almost two hours."

The train came to a complete stop and people began rummaging around, collecting the baggage they were able to carry into the passenger car.

"You might as well wait until most of the passengers vacate the car," he told Beverly. "We might be the last ones off the train, but we'll still get there right behind the rest of the people and we won't have to fight the crowd."

The group of girls grabbed their belongings and moved toward them, still talking. Thaddeus bent over to pull a small bag from under his seat when one of the girls let out a loud squeal.

"Oh, my gosh, I haven't seen one of these in years! May I?" she said, picking up Beverly's dime novel. "Where in the world did you find it? I thought it would be out of print by now." The girls crowded around to look at the cover.

"I bought it at Crown Books in Chicago, my favorite store."

Thaddeus looked up and sat transfixed, staring at the girl's crystal-clear blue eyes as Beverly asked, "Have you read the book?"

"Oh yes, many times."

Thaddeus finally found his voice and said, "I keep telling her the book is mostly fiction, and someone would be hard pressed to find any truth in it at all."

"And you would be right about parts of the book."

One of the boys stuck his head back through the door and yelled, "Hey, Caroline, you'd better get off the train, unless you want to go to the next town." Thaddeus slowly nodded. *The boys were traveling with the girls.* He wondered which one was this girl's boyfriend.

"Coming," she yelled back.

"I hope you're not trying to tell me the book is true," Thaddeus said with a snicker.

"No, what I am saying is, there is some truth in the book."

"Really? And how would you know which part is true and which part is fantasy?" He took the book from Beverly's hand and examined the cover as they exited the train. "You don't look like you're William Jefferson."

"No, I'm not the author."

"Then, answer my question. How would you know what's true and what isn't?"

"Because," she drug the word out slowly. "My mother is Victoria Jamison… well, it's Blue now. She married Matthew, making Matthew Blue my stepfather. My name is Caroline Blue. I was rather small when it all happened, but I was there, through the whole thing." She handed Beverly back her book and smiled at Thaddeus.

"Is that good enough for you, Mr. whatever your name is?"

Thaddeus was still staring at the girl as she collected her travel bag and squeezed into the line of passengers at the baggage claim. The city and railroad were in the process of having plans drawn to build a bigger and better station, but for now it was a battle between the workers and passengers trying to collect their baggage. As a result, they were crowded into a small area of the platform. The girls and boys she had been traveling with seemed to evaporate, leaving her to fend for herself.

"You're not going to help her?"

Thaddeus looked down at Beverly and shook his head with a grin.

"No, I don't think she likes me. I kind of made a jackass out of myself, didn't I?"

Beverly burst into giggles as they inched their way forward. "Yeah, but I've seen you do worse."

Chapter 2

Caroline admittedly felt a little guilty about being snippy with the young man, but she found his inquiry rather irritating, especially when her conversation was directed toward the girl he was traveling with, not him, and he was questioning her on whether what she was saying was true. She picked up her bag and brushed by him to collect the rest of her luggage. She had reached the loading dock when someone called her name several times.

"Caroline! Caroline!"

She turned to see Matthew weaving his way toward her.

"Daddy!" she squealed and ran toward him. Thaddeus thought the man must be around six-foot-four without an ounce of flab anywhere. The giant scooped her into his arms and spun her around like a rag doll.

Beverly brushed up against Thaddeus' arm and pointed. "That must be Manhunter."

"Who? What are you talking about?"

"Matthew Blue, her stepfather. Oh, I forgot. You didn't read the book." She gave him a crooked grin and picked up her bag.

"He just looks like an Indian to me," Thaddeus mumbled as he collected their suitcases. Thaddeus had never had a problem with Indians before, mainly because he had never lived around them much. He had seen a few Indians on a couple of business trips for their father, but he had never spoken to one of them, and the one swinging the pretty blond-headed girl in his arms didn't look like someone to be trifled with.

A young Indian boy, maybe thirteen years old, ran to give the girl a hug then picked up a couple of suitcases. He motioned with his head toward a buckboard parked on the outskirts of the crowd. A very attractive woman holding a young child was seated in the buckboard; she stood and hugged Caroline and kissed her on the cheek as she climbed inside the wagon.

"Come on," Beverly said as she half-drug her larger suitcase along the wooden dock. Caroline was already sitting in the rear seat of the buckboard beside the woman. They were talking animatedly while the boy and the man tossed the luggage into the bed. Matthew stopped to study one long, skinny pasteboard box and shook it before tucking it under the rear seat. The box took up the width of the wagon bed.

"Miss Blue? Miss Blue?" Beverly called loudly as a man backed into her, almost knocking her down.

"Hey, watch where you're going," Thaddeus barked as he caught Beverly in his arms. The man sized him up and down.

"It were an accident, boy. No harm done," the man said. He touched the brim of his hat then reached down to help Beverly with her suitcase. "This your rig?" He started to toss her luggage into the buckboard.

"No, thank you, sir," Beverly said. "I don't believe our wagon has arrived." As the man walked away, she took a deep breath to compose herself. "Miss Blue?"

"Yes? It's Beverly, isn't it? How may I help you?"

"I was wondering if you would please sign my book?"

"Certainly." She began rummaging inside her handbag and came out holding a fountain pin and a small bottle of ink. "As I said in the train, I haven't seen many copies of this book in the past few years." She scribbled a few words then passed the book to her mother and took the young girl from her lap.

"You might as well get my mother to sign it also. The book is about her anyway."

Vicky autographed the book then passed it to Matthew. "We can't forget Matthew. He's the one who saved our lives."

Matthew shrugged as he scribbled inside the book. "I hope it's okay. I've never signed a book before."

Beverly looked at their signatures then hugged the book against her breast.

"Oh, thank you so much."

"You should take good care of that book," Vicky said, with a laugh. "I think it's the only one with our signatures. It might make it worth a whole dollar or maybe even two someday."

"And what's your name, son?" Matthew said as he climbed into the buckboard.

"Thaddeus Josiah Jackson the Second, sir," Thaddeus said with a nod. Thaddeus decided to make a note of it in his calendar after they got checked into the hotel. It was the first time he could remember ever speaking to an Indian.

"Lord have mercy!" Matthew said, pushing his hat to the back of his head. "Depending on how long you plan on staying in this part of Kansas, I'd be shortening that name to something manageable, like Buck or Panhandle."

Thaddeus took a step backward and stared at him. Vicky laughed and retrieved her daughter from Caroline.

"Don't mind my husband, Mr. Jackson. He likes to joke around."

"Well, we'd best be leaving. We have a long drive ahead of us," Matthew said as he shook the reins. Thaddeus could hear him as the wagon pulled away.

"That wasn't all joking, Vicky. If that boy's gonna keep that name, he'd better get ready to be ribbed and maybe even goaded into a fight or two before it's over."

Thaddeus looked down at Beverly. "And we should find a spot to rent a buggy and check into a hotel."

"What do you think he meant by saying you'd better shorten your name, Thad?"

"I don't know, but I guess we'll find out."

Chapter 3

Jack Caldwell whistled and waved his lariat in an effort to keep the cows moving. He had been working for James Larkin for over a year now, and had decided this was what he intended to do for the rest of his life. Jim was an intelligent cattleman who read the newspapers and stayed abreast of world politics. Jim Larkin had a lot of money because of who he was, and Jack Caldwell wanted to form the same habits in his own life.

One other change Jack had decided to make was to marry Caroline Blue, the daughter of the local school teacher. He had decided it wasn't so much that she happened to be the prettiest girl in ten counties, but they had known each other for most of their lives. They had argued and fought and opposed each other whenever the teacher conducted a spelling bee or some other contest. His main problem, if he had one, was he couldn't picture his life without Caroline in it. He had been at the train station the day she left for finishing school and had counted each day until she returned. He had already picked out the rings in a Montgomery Ward catalogue and had saved enough money to pay cash when they arrived. He planned to ask her to be his bride the first chance he got. That was the day he got his first and only kiss from a girl other than his mother or sister. He hugged Caroline goodbye and she kissed him on the lips. It was just a little peck, but it was more than enough for him.

When he mentioned his feelings toward Caroline to Jim Larkin, the big man laughed and swatted him on the back.

"You'd best marry that girl the moment she comes back home Jack, 'cause every young buck from here to Mexico City will be trying to do the same thing."

He didn't know if that was true, because there were an awful lot of miles between Leon, Kansas and Mexico City. But Jim Larkin's warning fit right in with his plan. He stopped his horse and dismounted to study the tracks of a small herd of cattle that had crossed the road in front of them. Benjamin Polk rode up from the rear and dismounted beside him. The black *vaquero* was only a year older than Jack, but made a striking figure in his square-toed boots and brown high-brimmed hat.

"Huh," he said. "Reckon who they are?"

"I don't know," Jack said, scanning the horizon. "But this is Larkin's ranch, and he's not going to be very happy if they're stealing his cattle and horses."

"No, he won't be," John Larkin said as he dismounted. He was Jim's fifteen-year-old son who, in Jim's opinion, should be in school instead of herding cattle. His parents had more than one foot-stomping, yelling and cussing fight over the matter. But when Iris, Jim's wife, sided with her son, he'd relented and let John work for him, on the condition that he was just another cowboy working at the ranch. Jim declared if the boy wanted to be a cowboy, fine. But he had to learn what a real cowboy went through, including the pay.

"Well," Jack said as he stood to his feet. "Anybody got any ideas? What do we do now?"

"If it was up to me, I'd say we push this herd as hard as we can and once we've got the ranch in sight, then we send one of us in to tell Mr. Larkin about the tracks," Benjamin said.

"Sound's good to me, but those buzzards might say different." Jack pointed toward the east where a flock of vultures were circling.

"Dead cow?" John said, shading his eyes.

"I sure hope so," Jack said, climbing into the saddle.
"I've seen what those devils can do to a man and it isn't pretty. You guys bring the herd up toward the buzzards and I'll go check it out."

Jack pulled his Winchester from its scabbard as he trotted the bay quarter horse toward the circling birds. Watching them sink lower with each circle gave him a sick feeling in the pit of his stomach. He'd come upon a similar situation a year ago while driving a delivery wagon to El Dorado to pick up some special-order supplies that had come in on the train. He spied a flock of the black devils having a feast about a hundred yards or so off the road. Jack pulled the wagon aside, thinking he might report a dead steer or horse to the sheriff when he got to town. What he found though, was a drifter that the birds had almost stripped clean. About the only thing worth seeing were two of the birds fighting over a leg that still had some flesh on it. While they were fighting, a third bird landed on the limb and caused a bigger fight.

Jack took a deep breath and released it slowly. The birds were starting to collect around the body of a man who was lying face down. The deep, red tone of the grass told him that whoever it was had most likely bled to death right where he lay. Jack dismounted and yelled a few curses at two buzzards that had already landed and were hopping toward the body. One of the birds decided to hiss his displeasure at Jack's being there, so he shot him and rolled the body over as the sound of bawling cattle reached his ears.

"It's a man," he heard John Larkin yell. It took another minute for the young men to gather around Jack's side.

"Yeah. We all know him. It's Bob Sorenson."

"No! He's a good guy," John Larkin said with a catch in his voice. "Who'd want to hurt him?"

"Hurt him nothing," Benjamin Polk said with anger in his voice. "Whoever it was killed him. There wasn't any need of that."

"No, there wasn't," Jack stood and brushed his pant legs. "Why don't you guys toss a loop on that Appaloosa and bring him here. I don't want to leave Bobby laying out here like this." Jack surveyed the circling buzzards above their heads. "We were good friends most of our lives."

Benjamin and John walked back up the hill in silence as Jack dropped to his knees beside Sorenson's body, tears in his eyes.

Chapter 4

It had grown dark by the time the buckboard carrying Caroline and her family pulled into the yard with a barking dog. "Here, let me hold Rose while you get down," Caroline said as Vicky started to climb down. "You've got to start caring for my little brother."

"Really? I've conceived and done a fair job raising three children, counting you. I think I know a little about that subject."

Mark reached for one of the bags but Matthew stopped him.

"I'll get those, son. Why don't you go open up the house and light the lamp. Then, light the stove so your ma can cook supper."

"Yes sir."

The house was a far cry from the one-bedroom cabin that Matthew had built after he had married Prairie Flower. The tiny house was originally one room with a heavy curtain that divided off the sleeping quarters. Perhaps it was because Prairie Flower was full-blood Comanche, but she had never complained about the cabin being cramped for space, even after she had given birth to his son, Pita.

Matthew stopped and watched as Mark walked toward the house. He was now fourteen and growing into a fine lad. He'd like to think Pita would have been as tall and stout as Mark. He shook his head and continued unhitching the team. He seldom dwelt on Prairie Flower and Pita, as the thoughts depressed him.

Mark lit the kerosene lamp hanging over the table and had the wicks inside the kerosene stove roaring in a matter of minutes. He then rushed back outside to the barn and helped his father with the horses.

"You can go to the house and relax, Dad. I can care for the horses."

"Sure, I know you can. But if we both do it, we'll get it done in half the time," Mathew said with a grin. "We'll get roped into helping the women clean the dishes after we eat. Your ma's gotta teach school in the morning."

"I suppose that means I'll have to go also?"

"I suppose so, unless you can grow another year between now and the morning. One of the agreements I had to make if I was going to marry your mother was that we were not going to have ignorant children."

"Yeah, but it seems like a lot of wasted time to me." Mark poured grain into one of the feed troughs.

"Maybe so, but you'd better not let your ma or Caroline either one here you talk like that. Your ma's said time and again that her children were going to know how to read and write, and know something about the country they live in. You'd be surprised to know how little most white people know about their own country."

It only took a matter of minutes before the horses were taken care of. Mark poured a scoop of grain in the chicken pen on his way back to the house. Caroline had her large carpet bag opened and was busy passing out gifts.

"Here, Mark. This is for you."

"Oh, thank you." He unwrapped the small package, then cocked his head to one side with a grin. "What am I supposed to do with it?"

"What do you mean, '*what am I supposed to do with it?*' It's an inkwell and a very nice pen," Caroline said with a scowl.

"Yeah, I know what it is. I just can't see me sitting at the table writing letters to a bunch of people I hardly know." Mark shrugged and raised his eyebrows.

"Well, it's evident I forgot to teach you some manners," Vicky said as she dumped a bowl of sliced potatoes into a heated frying pan.

"It's okay, Mama. I thought he might act that way." Caroline leaned across the table and glared at her brother. "You can believe me, Mark. There will come a day when you'll be glad your mother spent as much time as she did teaching you."

"Oh, I already am. I just can't see myself sitting at this table writing letters to people I don't even know."

"Maybe not," Caroline said as she removed a small box with a ribbon from her carpet bag and handed it to Vicky. "Here, Mama. This is for you."

"Oh!" Vicky said as she removed the lid to reveal a dozen crocheted and monogrammed handkerchiefs. She only had two handkerchiefs left from what her grandmother had given her as a wedding present, and they were never this nice when they were new.

"Thank you, thank you, thank you," she said between kissing Caroline's cheeks. "They're almost too good to use… but I will."

"And this is for you, Dad." Caroline handed him the beat-up pasteboard box.

"What's in it?" Matthew shook the box.

"Open it, silly man," Vicky said as she slid a pan of biscuits into the oven. It took a moment of trying to save the box before Matthew pulled his knife and sliced the box apart. He stared at the contents for a few seconds before holding them in the air.

"Is this what I think it is?"

"I don't know, Dad. What do you think it is?"

"It looks like a very large bow with a quiver of arrows."

"And that is exactly what it is." Caroline rounded the table and pulled the quiver from the box.

"One of the lecturers at the school was an old man born and raised in Wales. I loved his class." She stared at the wall with a blank expression for a few seconds before shaking her head. "Anyway, he was retiring and selling most of his collection of teaching aids. When he discovered my father was a Comanche, and I said you would love to see it, he gave it to me to give to you." She laid the arrows on the table and began crumpling up the box and paper. "It's an English longbow, made out of yew wood. It has a pull of almost 150 pounds, and has an effective range of 350 yards."

"Really? That far?"

"According to the professor, yes it really does," Caroline said.

"Huh," Mark said and he ran his fingers down one of the arrows. "Makes you wonder what Quanah Parker and his braves would have done if they were armed with these."

"You can believe things would have turned out the same." Vicky slid the frying pan to a cooler part of the stove. "Now, if you'll clean and set the table, we'll eat.

****

Matthew crawled out of bed well before daylight. He fed and watered the animals as Tippy, Caroline's dog, hobbled along behind him. The mongrel was well past ten years old, and while he had survived the attack of a lion, the poor old guy had never fully rebounded. Matthew squatted to pet the dog, and ruffled his ears.

"Yeah, I know. Time is getting kind of short for you, isn't it? I've felt the flutter of angel's wings myself a few times. If they come for you any time soon, just make sure Caroline's not here. She still thinks the sun rises and sets in you." The dog whimpered and licked Matthew's hand, so he cut a hunk of elk jerky and gave it to him.

"Don't tell Vicky I gave you that, or I'll never hear the end. She thinks you need a healthy diet… whatever that is. Women don't understand us men as well as they think they do."

He pulled a work bench away from the wall before unrolling a strip of rawhide. He had noticed the bowstring on the English bow that Caroline had given him was ready to fall apart. Using the old string as a pattern, he cut three new strings before coating them with beeswax then attaching them to the bench. He then began the slow, tedious process of braiding them into one six-foot string capable of handling the 150-pound pull. He paused every now and then to add more wax and stretch the string. He could smell fresh-brewed coffee and bacon long before Mark came to fetch him to breakfast.

"What were you doing inside the barn so early this morning? Is anything wrong?" Vicky asked as she slid a mug of coffee in front of Matthew and kissed him.

"Oh, I noticed the string on the bow Caroline gave me has a bad spot in it, so I thought I'd make a new string."

"That's nice," Vicky said. "I have a feeling that bow is quite old."

"I thought so." He smiled at her and took a bite of bacon.

"Matthew Blue!" She scowled at him with her hands on her hips.

"Why? What'd I do?"

"What did you do? You're eating bacon without us asking the blessing."

"Oh." He wiped his fingers on the cotton napkin and grinned.

******

Matthew and Mark had just finished hooking the team of horses to the wagon when Cotton and Jim Larkin rode into the yard. Cotton removed his brown hat and nodded his grey head as Caroline came out onto the porch.

"Howdy, Carol. It's good to see you made it home okay."

"Well, hello, Cotton… Jim," Vicky said as she exited the door on Caroline's heels. "What brings you all the way out here?"

"You can bet it's nothing good." Mathew patted the horse on the rump as he rounded the wagon.

"Well, just to set the record straight, no it ain't good news that brought us out," Jim Larkin said.

"No, it isn't." Cotton said as he dismounted. "Someone decided to rustle about thirty head from Jim's herd yesterday and killed Bobby Sorenson in the process. It happened sometime yesterday afternoon."

"No!" Caroline cried. "You're lying to me. Everybody loved Bobby."

"I'm sorry you had to hear about it this way, Carol. I know that you and Jack Caldwell always had Bobby with you, whatever you were doing.

Caroline ran into the house and sat in one of the kitchen chairs facing a corner with her back toward everyone else.

"Where's Dave? I thought he was the sheriff now that you're retired. Or, are you taking it all back, since you've got some rustlers to catch?" Matthew lit a cigarette.

"No, Dave's back at Leon forming a posse. He asked me to get you to join them," Cotton said with a snort. "I'd like to join them myself, but that blasted doctor's sided with Alice and they're ganging up on me. It's up to you now."

"Time's critical, Matt," Jim Larkin said with a rumble.

"Time's always critical, Jim." Matthew snorted. "Got any idea where they're headed?"

"Yeah, I've got an idea. They cut a trail across the backside of my property, leaving some of the prettiest tracks you ever saw." Jim Larkin pulled a couple of cigars from his shirt pocket and passed one of them to Matthew.

"So, you coming?" Jim struck a match against the corral fence and lit his cigar, then held the match for Matthew.

"Sure." Matthew released a cloud of smoke and nodded. I don't know if it'll do much good, but I'll come."

"What do you mean you don't know what good it'll do? You're the best tracker around here," Jim Larkin barked.

"True, but by your own admission the theft took place yesterday, and here we are today, a good five miles or more from your ranch, discussing what we think happened. That's not very good odds, Jim."

"Yeah, well things might be better than we think," Cotton said as he climbed back onto his horse. "We've got three men on the posse who came up on Bobby's body not too long after he'd been killed."

"Well, thank God for small miracles." Matthew entered a corral that contained several horses and chose a large brown and white paint. The horse followed him out of the pen and stood silently waiting while Matthew threw a saddle on him.

"How's that, Matt?"

"How's what?"

"You said *thank God for small miracles.* Someone stole around thirty head and shot Bobby Sorenson dead. I haven't seen a whole lot to be thankful for."

"You said we had a set of pretty good tracks. We *could* be starting with nothing. I would suggest you and

Cotton get back into town and tell that posse to stay away from the tracks until I'm there; It's going to take me a few minutes to pack my grip and check on my daughter."

Cotton grinned and turned his horse in a tight circle.

"Come on, Jim, he's liable to beat us back into town as it is."

Chapter 5

"There ain't none around here, son." The grizzled old man who ran the mercantile snorted and shook his head.

"You're joking. We saw quite a few horses just walking a few blocks from the depot to your store." Thaddeus was almost ready to write the man down as being lazy or just plain crazy.

"Sure, you probably spied quite a few horses out there." He set a tin of pipe tobacco on the counter and checked the item off a list then moved to another aisle.

"The trouble you're having is all them oil rigs you find out there. All it took was for old man Norman over in Wilson County to allow one of those outfits to drill a test well on his ranch." He pulled out two cans of coffee and placed them on the counter.

"Then what happened?" Beverly said.

"Well, I'll tell you what happened, missy." The clerk grunted as he hefted a large sack of flour onto the floor below the order he'd been working on then leaned against the counter to catch his breath.

"What happened was the drilling outfit struck plenty of oil, then everyone else wanted in on the deal. Most of the ranches and farms around here sold off their cattle and livestock in order to drill for oil. We used to have some pretty nice farms and ranches, but you'd really have to look to find one. Why? You looking to go into the cattle business or something?"

"Yes, actually I am… for our father." Thad shook the old man's hand. "Name's Thad Jackson."

"Webster Plummer. You say your pa wants to buy some horses? How many?"

He wants to buy a lot of horses." Thad cocked his head to one side and grinned. "Where do I have to go to find some horses?"

"Well, I'd say head over to Leon and talk to Jim Larkin or Matthew Blue. There's others, but Larkin and Blue both raise and sell quality horses."

"This Matthew Blue wouldn't happen to have a pretty blond-headed daughter, would he?" Beverly tried choking back a laugh.

"Yes, he does. He's got several young-uns, but that girl's his oldest. Why? Have you met them already?"

"Yes, we have." Beverly almost doubled over laughing. "And my brother just happened to insult her in the process."

"Really?" The old man snorted. "I've met her before. Well, actually, I know the whole family." He hoisted the larger sack of flour back onto the counter. "They're all really nice folks. I never figured any one of 'em needed insulting."

"Evidently my brother thought so." Beverly laughed and skipped away from Thaddeus' reach.

"Well, both of you can laugh at me if you want. But the man at the ticket booth said a bridge between El Dorado and Leon is washed out and we're going to be in real trouble if we can't find a buggy or a place to stay this evening. What do you suggest we do?"

"What I suggest you do is rent yourself a room at the boarding house across the street. Rooms are kind of high, but Wanda doesn't charge for breakfast or supper, so it kind of makes up for it. Then in the morning, check back with me. Most of that order on the counter's going to the Richardsons who own the hotel in Leon. Depending on how big a load Smokey has, you just might be able to hitch a ride to Leon."

"Thank you, sir," Thaddeus said, shaking the old man's hand. He scooped Beverly into his arms and dashed across the muddy street, wondering why it took the old goat so long to say what he did. Beverly giggled as he placed her on the walkway in front of a restaurant. A woman who had just crossed the street in front of them punched her husband in the arm and pointed toward Thaddeus. "See? That's what I've been talking about. That young man is a real gentleman." The couple wandered down the sidewalk arguing.

"Thank you, Thaddeus. It's been so long since you picked me up, I thought you'd forgotten how."

"Don't get too used to the idea," he said brushing a wrinkle from his jacket. "You're getting too big to be carried around."

"See, there you go again, being a snot!" Beverly gave him a gentle shove. "Why do you have to be that way?"

"What?" he said, holding the restaurant door open for her. "I just stated a fact. You're at that wonderful age of being a kid and a grown woman at the same time. Pretty soon it will be acceptable for another young man to carry you across muddy streets, but not me, being your brother.

"Why? That's a silly rule," Beverly said as she sat in the chair Thaddeus had pulled away from the table.

"That, my dear sister, I don't know. That's just the way it is."

A loud whistle made them both jump as a portly woman approached their table and laughed. "Let me guess. You two just got into town on the noon train."

"Yes, we did," Beverly said. "What was that?"

"The 4:00 o'clock whistle. It lets the men working in the oilfield know that it's time to switch shifts. Well, they call it an oil field, but so far, they've only found salt water. What can I get you two?"

"A good cup of coffee for me," Thaddeus said as he studied a menu.

"I'll take the same," Beverly said, giving the menu a quick once over.

"Two coffees it is. Either one of you want cream and sugar in your coffees?"

"I do," Beverly said.

"Just black for me." Thaddeus scooted his chair back and seemed to relax all at once. The door opened and some men who looked like they'd bathed in mud entered and grabbed chairs at the next table. They studied Beverly from top to bottom. She smiled back and gave her brother a sideways glance, which he ignored.

"Okay, what can I get you guys?" the waitress said to the men at the next table.

"I'll take the Driller's Special," one of the men said.

They sipped their coffees slowly as several other men entered the restaurant. Thad finally pushed his empty cup toward the center of the table.

"I guess we'd better go find a room," Thaddeus said as he stood. He left more than enough money at the table and thanked the waitress. They drug their luggage to the boarding house next door where the woman behind a small counter lowered her eyeglasses as she gave them a wide grin.

"Well, you're sure not from these parts. My name's Wanda. What can I do for you?"

"We need a couple of rooms, hopefully for one night," Thaddeus said, dropping his bag with a soft thud.

"I can give you one room for two nights."

"No, we'd both like our own rooms, if possible."

"I'm sure you do, the same as the last couple that was in here an hour ago, but all I have left is one room for two nights. Besides, why wouldn't a young groom like you want to sleep in the same bed with his bride?"

"Oh, we're not married. He's my brother," Beverly said with a giggle.

"Well, you just got married and have a real nice room on the first floor. I can provide extra blankets and towels. Breakfast and dinner come with the room." She spun the ledger around and gave them a crooked grin. "You won't find a cleaner room in El Dorado."

"Come on, Thad. I'm getting tired of dragging this luggage around," Beverly said.

"Okay, you fill out the register. How much?"

"Two dollars, Mr. and Mrs… ," she leaned to read the register, "Jackson. You're in room two, right down the hall. I'd recommend using the bath early, as it does get busy every evening."

******

Thaddeus was seated at a small table making notes in a black ledger when Beverly came from behind the dressing screen brushing her long, black hair. She was dressed in a long pink gown and matching slippers.

"What are you doing, brother?"

"Just making notes on our expenditures so dad can see what we're up against. Who would have believed we'd have trouble finding horses in El Dorado, Kansas."

"Yeah, but tomorrow we're heading to Leon. Maybe we'll find exactly what he's looking for there."

"Let's hope so." Thaddeus stood to stretch his lanky body. "Dad gets rather impatient when things don't go his way."

"Yes, I know that he does." Beverly took his place at the table and pointed. "You can have the screen now. I promise not to peek."

"Thanks." Thaddeus grabbed his pajamas from his carpet bag and stopped to look back at her. "Uh, maybe you'd like to come remove your unmentionables first.

Chapter 6

Andrew Thomas stood on the wooden sidewalk holding a corn broom in his hand. The young girl with long, dark brown hair had just left his shop carrying a pound of ground beef wrapped in heavy butcher's paper. It was starting already. The bridge washed out and the sale of perishable things like fresh meat and dairy products didn't just slow down. Depending on the financial backing, in some cases they quit altogether. The girl had just purchased a pound of his finest, but with the slowly melting ice inside his cool room, he just might need to close his door early.

He took a couple more swipes with the broom when Sheriff Dave Price ambled toward him.

"Hello, Andrew. How's business going?"

"It ain't, sheriff. I had a couple of elderly coffee drinkers this morning. Then, that girl in the blue dress across the street came in a few minutes ago and bought a pound of ground beef. Then Alice Blankenship bought a pound of bacon, and a couple of people bought some sausage."

"Is that it?"

"That's it. I've got about two days of ice left, and I'll have to feed coyotes good Kansas beef."

"Well, let's hope it doesn't turn to that. I'll see you around, Andrew."

Sheriff Price started moving when Andrew stopped him.

"Hey, Sheriff. What's that girl's name?"

"Who? The girl in the blue dress?"

"Yeah, that's the one."

"Oh, that's Mary Turner. She manages the library, and her brother manages the hotel. Her Pa, Fred, used to work at the bank. He had a stroke about a month ago. Why?"

"No reason. She just seemed like a nice sort. Too bad all young people couldn't be more like her."

"Yeah, I think you're right."

Andrew smiled as he went about his sweeping while Dave Price crossed the street toward the coffee shop. It was too bad the sheriff nor anyone else in the city limits seemed to care about the bruised left cheekbone on the girl's face. That was okay though. Andrew was familiar with those types of wounds and knew how to erase the pain that went with them.

Chapter 7

Thad felt a mixture of pride and anger as several young cowboys stopped unloading a buckboard in front of the general store and stared as Beverly hiked her dress to mid-ankle and crossed the street beside Thad. Thad stopped on the sidewalk to glare at the men before entering the store.

"Don't go blaming them," Beverly said. "They wouldn't be gawking if you would have carried me across the street."

"What makes you say that?"

"They would have thought I belonged to you. But since you were ignoring me, they're wondering if I'm free."

"Well, they can keep their eyes to themselves because you're only fourteen and not available."

Webster Plummer was scribbling in a ledger and looked up when they entered the store.

"There you are. I was beginning to wonder if you'd found another ride."

"No sir. We were enjoying Wanda's pancakes and eggs," Thad said.

"Well come follow me. I've got someone I want you to meet."

They followed him down one isle before turning toward the back of the store. Beverly felt her heart rate increase as they stopped by a kerosene-burning stove where a grizzled old man was pouring himself a cup of coffee. He looked just like some of the illustrations inside her dime novels, with long grey hair that hung past his shoulders, and a grey beard that hung to his stomach.

"Smokey? These are the folks that need a ride to Leon. Reckon you can accommodate them?"

Smokey set the pot back on the stove and took a long sip from his mug as he eyed them both up and down.

"I reckon I might. But they might wanna change into something besides what they've got on."

"Oh, I didn't think of that, but Smokey's right," Webster said.

"Why? Is the road a rough one?" Thad said as Beverly tried to examine herself.

"No, they's pretty good roads… considering. It's just the time of the year. With them clouds hanging around, we could run into some more rain and this old buckboard has a habit of tossing mud around. It could mess up them fancy things you have on." Smokey took another sip from his mug. "Best get to it. I'll be leaving in a jiffy."

"Okay," Thad said holding out his right hand. "We'll get our gear and change. Don't leave without us."

He grabbed Beverly by the hand and rushed her out of the store, where he scooped her into his arms and skipped across the street. He paid for both nights, figuring a room to sleep in and breakfast for two and transportation to Leon was still cheap. Beverly had changed into a dark-brown riding skirt with a white blouse and jacket a that fit her perfectly. Thad figured they were on a tight time schedule, so he bit his tongue and carried their luggage across the street first, then went back to get Beverly.

"What?" she said as he scooped her into his arms and started across the street.

"You could have dressed more modestly."

"Thad," she laughed, "this was all I had."

"You have more clothes than the Emporium back in Chicago."

"True, but I had no idea what to bring. Besides," she added as he placed her on the sidewalk. "It looks like you didn't do much better." She backed away from him and snickered.

Thad glanced at his reflection in the window and had to admit she was right. He had always thought it a waste of time to stop what you were doing to make a choice about what clothing to wear. What he had on was pretty much like what he'd worn yesterday and the day before. He couldn't wait to get back to Chicago where things were somewhat normal.

"Is she yours?"

"I beg your pardon," Thad said to the young cowboy leaning against the buckboard rolling a cigarette.

"I asked if the young woman was yours. You know, your wife or girlfriend."

"No. She's my sister."

"No kidding." He struck a match against the buckboard and lit his cigarette. "Then, is it alright if I come calling on her?"

"No, I'd rather you didn't."

"Why not? Not good enough?"

"No, class or social standing has nothing to do with it. She's only fourteen, and way too young to be seeing men. But it doesn't really matter since we're leaving El Dorado as soon as we can get the man called Smokey out here."

"That may take a while," one of the other men said with a laugh.

"Aw come on, guys. You're scaring the folks."

In a matter of seconds, the four men were laughing and joking about the reliability of the driver and kept at it until Smokey appeared.

"Well, great day in the morning, Smokey," said the cowboy that had asked to see Beverly.. "The way you was sitting by the coffee pot, I figured you was dead. It's good to see you're still alive."

"Now, now, boys. Respect your elders," Smokey said as he looked inside the bed. He then turned to Thad. "The bags against the wall your grip?"

"Yes, it is."

"Well better toss it in the bed, unless you want to run around Leon naked."

Thad grabbed one of the bags with the intention of tossing it into the buckboard but one of the cowboys took it from his hands.

"I've got this." He handed the bag to one of the other men who had climbed into the bed. In a matter of seconds their baggage was secure inside the buckboard and tucked under a waterproof tarp.

Smokey used one of the front wheels on the buckboard as a ladder to get in the rig, then turned to help Beverly. The four cowboys all jockeyed for a position to ``help her into the rig. She turned and smiled at the men.

"Okay, I would like to know your names. You are…?" She pointed.

"I'm Rio, ma'am." He removed his hat and bowed slightly.

"And you are?"

"Folks call me Arizona, 'cause that's where I was born."

"And you?"

"I'm Preacher, ma'am, 'cause my pa's a real one back in Tennessee."

"He's got some good learning, if you can stand it," Rio said with a laugh.

"And what's your name?"

"Folks just call me Bill, 'cause that's the name my pa gave me."

"It's a very good name. I hope to see you men again before I return home."

"Oh, I'm sure once we figure where you set up camp, we'll show up and swap howdies," Rio said.

Beverly squeezed into the seat between Smokey and her brother. Smokey shook the reins and called out to the mules.

"Yah! Sandy! Fancy! Get up there or I'll let the Comanche have your ornery hides."

The buckboard lurched forward as one of the mules brayed.

"Keep your eyes peeled 'cause you're gonna see some real beautiful country."

"How far is this Leon? I had never heard of it until yesterday from Webster at the store." Thad grabbed Beverly as the buckboard hit a hole and bounced her in the air.

"Leon? Aw, not too far. A little over twelve miles. We should reach it mid to late afternoon. Depends on the weather and what not."

The buckboard rolled and rattled its way toward Leon. Smokey called for a rest about halfway, then loaded them back into the wagon and resumed. He gave them a good view of Kansas history that Thad was positive had been embellished by the memory of an old man who loved to talk and swap stories with other old men around a campfire as a bottle was being passed. Beverly covered her mouth and wretched when Smokey talked about a grasshopper infestation that stripped the leaves from trees and left starving people as well as cattle.

"Yeah, there weren't nothing for folks to eat, so most of the folks started frying up the critters. They figured since the hoppers ate their food they'd eat the hoppers." Smokey shook his head slowly. "That was in the summer of '74. The little devils ate the shirt right off my back."

"How did you get rid of them?" Thad said.

"I don't know if the folks around here had much of an effect on getting rid of them. I think once all the food was gone, the hoppers just up and moved on. Well, there's Leon." Smokey pointed.

The picturesque little town came into view as the wagon rounded a bend in the road and Smokey stopped the buckboard in the middle of the street to stare at the milling crowd.

"Something's wrong." He leaned to spit over the side of the rig, then wiped his lips with the back of his left glove.

"What's wrong?" Beverly sat up straight, staring at the crowd.

"That, I don't know. Y'all just wait right here 'til I can figure it out. It don't look too good."

Smokey disappeared into the crowd. Beverly stood and stretched, trying to spot Smokey.

"What do you think happened, Thad?"

"I don't know, but you'd better sit back down."

"I'm sick of riding in this thing."

"Me too, but you'd better sit. If something happened to startle those mules, it might cause you to fall over the side and really get hurt."

Beverly put on her best pouty look as she plopped to the seat. She had been sitting for a couple of minutes before Smokey returned and climbed back into the seat.

"What's going on?" Thad said.

"From what I figure, some rustlers stole a small herd from Jim Larkin and killed one of his drovers. I'd say stick tight. Folks are kind of upset right now. Yah, Sandy, Fancy! Get up there."

Smokey walked the mules toward the general store and parked the rig. "You'd better climb out right here. The hotel is right over there, across the street. You might check for a room there. If they're out, there's a couple of boarding houses at the edge of town that-a-way." He pointed toward the opposite end of town.

Smokey climbed back into the rig and handed Thad their luggage. As they crossed the street Thad looked back. A couple of people had come from inside the store to help Smokey unload the wagon. They passed a group of four men sharing a bottle, who gave Beverly a look that caused his blood to boil. He held the door open as Beverly passed.

"It appears you have a knack for drawing trouble."

She gave him a crooked grin and dropped her suitcase on the carpet.

Chapter 8

Caroline dried her eyes, then started rummaging through boxes. She was sure she had gained several pounds while being away at school. It would be interesting to see what might still fit clothing-wise, and what might be useful. It wasn't that she didn't trust her father or Dave or Uncle Harvey to bring the rustlers in for justice. But she wanted to be standing there, dressed appropriately, watching as they slipped a rope around the killer's neck.

She doubted very much that her finishing school teacher, Rebecca Grayson, would approve of her even thinking such a thing, but Rebecca Grayson didn't know Bobby Sorenson. Caroline did know him well. They'd competed against each other every chance they got. Jack Caldwell, Caroline Blue and Bobby Sorenson were the best of friends. They rode horses, played ball and fished. No, Rebecca Grayson could never understand the way she felt.

She pulled two Comanche buckskin dresses from a box and held the newer of the two against her body as she stood in front of a mirror. Mathew had given it to her just before she left for school. It had never been worn and looked in perfect condition. She found the knife Matthew had given her with the scabbard in the bottom of the box along with the beaded headband. The beaded moccasins were a little loose to begin with, so they should be fine. Comanche women go pretty much natural under their dress, so that part was easy.

Caroline stood in the middle of the room and stripped down to her underwear, then removed most of that. A few moments later she was standing in front of a mirror, evaluating the image staring back.

The last item in the box was a small container of bright red clay. Caroline added a few drops of water and stirred before dipping her finger in the clay and making a single red stripe across her nose from cheek to cheek. She then stuffed the clothing she'd removed back into the box and braided her hair into two pigtails. Satisfied with the image looking back at her, Caroline folded and repacked the boxes then ran to the corral.

Her family had gone into town right after the visit from Uncle Harvey and Jim Larkin, so there was no one to impede her progress. She chose a small buckskin mare she had named Laughing Brook, after the name of the Comanche princess who gave it to her. Laughing Brook's husband, Three Horns, and her father had grown up together and were the best of friends before he died. The horse stomped its feet and whinnied while Caroline locked the corral.

"You remember me, don't you girl? There wasn't a day that went by that I didn't think of you."

Caroline placed a bit into its mouth and hugged the horse around the neck. She kissed its cheek before grabbing a fistful of mane and leaping on the horse's back. Caroline turned the buckskin to the right, then back to the left.

"Yah!" Caroline patted her neck before digging her heels into Laughing Brook's sides. "Let's go!"

The horse darted down the trail. Given the time that her mother had left the ranch, Caroline figured they would be about halfway to town. She would more than likely pitch a grand old fit when she saw her, but that would be okay. Caroline could live with that. This ride was for Bobby.

They were approaching a fork in the road and Caroline guided the horse to the right. Laughing Brook seemed to be reaching a comfortable gait, so Caroline gave her more rein and the animal picked up speed. The road they were following led to the back pasture on Jim Larkin's ranch. While the road cut off several miles, it was rough, with several large washes, and was loaded with rocks and brush, making it impossible for wagons. Caroline pulled back on the reins and slowed the horse. They were approaching another fork in the road. She took the fork toward the left, which led to the back door of Thomas's Meat Market in the middle of town.

They crossed the bottom of the first wash, splashing through a small stream. She allowed Laughing Brook to indulge herself with a small drink before urging her up the opposite side, where she again picked up speed. An antelope poked his head up from the depth of the second wash about fifty yards ahead and darted away. Allowing her mind to drift, Caroline tried to format questions she wanted to ask Uncle Harvey about Bobby's death. Her father would talk to her, but he had some sort of inner rule that would only allow him to tell her what he thought she needed to know. Harvey, on the other hand, had been a lawman most of his life and stuck by the rule of law no matter what. He had been accused of being too blunt and maybe a little crass at times. But you always got the truth and knew how things set.

Caroline came out of the fourth wash and reined Laughing Brook to a halt. Four Comanche braves sat on horseback in the middle of the trail. Their leader was a large black man, who grinned and nudged his pony forward then spoke in Comanche.

"Good morning, little princess. I see they haven't stolen your magic while you were away."

"No, I would not let them, Shadow." Caroline dismounted and sat on her heels, inviting Shadow and the braves to join her. There had been rumors of the cruelty of a runaway slave who had joined White Cloud's band of Kwa Hadi Comanche, but Caroline had always found the claims to be false. The Shadow she knew was a kind, gentle man, and she refused to listen to claims otherwise. It was Cotton who took her aside one day and opened her eyes.

"All I'm asking is for you to be very careful around him. Shadow's been beaten and abused a million different ways, and as big and strong as he is, it wouldn't take much for him to really hurt or even kill someone."

"You're quite a distance from the reservation, Shadow. Is there something wrong?"

"There is always something wrong on the reservation," Shadow said with a laugh.

"Yes, I suppose that's true. What are they doing now?"

"I think they are trying to starve us. There are too many people and the agent is supposed to buy cattle from local ranchers and give it to us to eat. What they are really doing is writing a higher amount of cattle sold in the ledger than what the rancher delivers. Then, the white man's government pays the agent for the full amount of cattle they ordered and he pockets the extra money."

"And I suppose," Caroline smirked, "It would be hard to lodge a complaint, since you'd have to go through the agent to do so. That's fraud."

"Yes, you are right, Princess. Now, what has you out here looking like you're on the warpath?"

"Someone stole about thirty head of cattle from Jim Larkin's place and killed a good friend of mine in the process."

"They'll blame it on us because we left the reservation to hunt food." The comment came from a brave known as Low Dog and caused the others to laugh.

"Well, I'd better go see if I can find out something about Bobby's death." Caroline rose to her feet. "When they catch whoever it is, I'll tell Sheriff Blankenship about your agent. It would be good to stick him inside a prison with people he's starved."

"That will never happen." Shadow laughed loudly. "Ride well, Princess. And always check where you've been."

Caroline watched as the Indians dropped into the wash and seemed to disappear. She mounted Laughing Brook and urged the pony into a full run toward town without slowing when she crossed the final wash. It was a mile from the last wash to Leon, and Thomas's Meat Market.

******

Caroline left Laughing Brook on a patch of grass at the rear of the store and slipped silently toward the front without anyone noticing. She stopped at a small corral where Thomas had a green hide hanging on the railing. The brand on the left flank happened to be Jim Larkin's JL brand. Caroline looked around before pulling her knife and cutting the brand out. She had no idea what Andrew Thomas was doing with one of Jim Larkin's hides but she would let her father and Dave Price worry about it.

Harvey and her father were both standing at the edge of a group of men and women calling for some sort of justice. Dave Price was now sheriff, since Harvey had supposedly retired, but Caroline saw little difference in the way things were being done. Everything had its own place and reason for being. She slid with her back against the wall and inched her way toward Harvey.

She was almost to the opposite corner when she looked up to see her father watching her. He grinned and looked back at the crowd only to lose her again.

"Okay," Dave yelled, quieting the crowd. "We have the posse chosen. If you're a member of the posse, be here at sunrise tomorrow. We will leave as early as possible. The rest of you, stay home and take care of your families."

Dave fielded questions as Harvey tapped Matthew on the arm and motioned for him to follow him toward Dave's office.

"Well, I'm glad my eyes aren't failing me," Harvey said as they worked their way inside. "I thought that was you out there. I see you've got your war paint on. Any specific reason?"

"Yes; I want to be part of the posse."

"Well," Harvey drug the word out, "women usually aren't members of a posse."

"Yes, I know. I was there this morning when you and Jim Larkin came and got my dad without offering to use me. I can track. My dad showed me."

"That may be," Harvey said as he sat in Dave's chair with a grunt. "But tracking deer and horses is different. Deer and horses don't carry guns and shoot back."

"That's what you're worried about? Me getting shot at?"

"Harvey's just trying to keep you alive, Caroline," Matthew said as he started a fresh pot of coffee. Dave Price came in with Albert Meeks, who took a chair. Dave stood staring at Harvey as the man leaned back in his chair.

"Grab a chair, son. This office has more than one."

"I know it does. That squeaking thing you're sitting in happens to be mine."

"Not today, it doesn't. And tomorrow you'll be leading a posse, so who cares?"

"I'll care, that's who. You're sitting in my chair."

"And just as soon as you catch these rustlers and the killer, I'll give you back your chair. But as long as they're still on the loose, you should be out looking for them."

"Are you going with the posse, Dave?" Caroline said as she took a seat along the opposite wall.

"Yes, I am. Are you going?"

"No, my dad and Uncle Harvey won't let me. They say it's too dangerous."

"Well… it is dangerous, I'll grant you that. The last posse I was on, we got shot at several times."

"There are a lot of things that are dangerous, Dave. Hunting and fishing are dangerous, but people do them every day."

"Yes, but people who are fishing in the river don't have your mother ready to skin 'em alive if you got hurt or died. The answer is 'no.' I can't let you be a member of the posse."

Caroline's face grew red as she ground her teeth.

"Don't pay them any mind," Harvey said with a chuckle. "I'm glad they won't let you go with them. Now, I can use you to find some important information."

"Such as?" Dave said.

"Such as how did the thieves get on the Larkin Ranch?"

"Why do we need to know that?" Albert Meeks asked.

"Most thieves and rustlers will want to grab whatever it is they are stealing and get out of there quickly." Matthew paused to lick the cigarette he had just rolled. "If you can establish where they came from, you should have an idea who you're dealing with."

"Huh," Albert said thoughtfully. "That makes sense. I've never thought of it that way before. But are you sure about discussing it in front of Matthew?" Albert laughed and leaned away as Matthew swatted at him.

"Why not? He's the one who told me about it," Harvey said with a snort. "Regardless, Carol doesn't need to worry about being involved in finding Bobby's murderer. We'll use her every chance we get. The same as you guys."

******

Sweat trickled down Andrew Thomas' cheeks and collected on his white pullover shirt and butcher's apron as he paced the stone and mortar floor in his shop. It wasn't supposed to happen this way. They were just going to pop in and pop out really quick. No one was even going to see them and no one was supposed to get hurt. To his dying day, Andrew would never know what the Sorenson kid was doing on that part of the Larkin Ranch. He was supposed to be at the main house, painting the barn. But, just as sure as you're born, Bobby Sorenson shows up cutting their trail.

At first, Andrew was going to ignore him, thinking he'd just go away, or at the least, go tell Larkin they were stealing his cattle. He figured if that happened, he could lie his way out of the situation and make Larkin think Bobby didn't really see what he saw. But the stupid idiot pulled a gun on him. The next instant, he was staring at Bobby's body lying on the recent trail that thirty head of cattle had just made.

Rustling was something Andrew would not have fooled with, but the lifestyle he had chosen took a lot of money and Andrew was down to his last dime.

"Hey, boss. We'd best be going. I'm sure they heard that forty-four all the way to the main house," Waco said as his pony danced around Andrew's horse. "Boss?" he repeated himself. "We'd better get going."

Andrew turned his horse and followed Waco and his friends down into a wash toward the little rundown ranch he owned.

Chapter 9

Thaddeus gripped Beverly's arm and wove a small trail through the people gathered in front of the sheriffs' office, which resulted in a crowd in front of the hotel. Someone told him they had just finished selecting a posse to hunt down a band of rustlers, and expected trouble. The whole idea seemed to excite Beverly, but caused Thad to wonder if there wasn't somewhere safer to buy his father's horses.

Thad made his way to the reception desk. A midsized man with eyeglasses pinching the tip of his nose looked up from the stack of mail he was sorting and smiled.

"Good afternoon. I'm surprised that you made it through that crowd out there. It's a real zoo." He poked his hand over the desk to shake Thad's hand. "Randal Turner at your service. What can I do for you folks?"

"We'd like two adjoining rooms, if possible."

"Two rooms?"

"Yes, it seems most people around here think we're married, but we're actually brother and sister." Beverly flashed a brilliant smile at the man. Thad thought she probably could have convinced him they had just arrived from the moon if she wanted.

"Two rooms… yes, I have two lovely adjoining rooms on the second floor. If you'd just sign the register, and I'll get your keys for you."

"Also," Thad said as he scribbled in the ledger, "do you have a safe for customers staying here?"

"Yes, we sure do." He reached under the counter and produced a lockbox with the room number painted on its side and a key. "You just put what you want saved in here and lock it with the key, then I place it in the large vault in the office."

"And you're sure it's safe there?"

"Oh, yes sir. It's as safe here as it is inside the bank."

Beverly noticed the four men whom they had spied drinking standing next to the door, watching them.

Thad unzipped his carpet bag and removed the envelope from his father. He laid it on the counter then removed a couple of bills and placed them inside his billfold before retying the envelope closed and placing it inside the lockbox.

"You're sure it's safe in here."

"Oh, yes. Totally safe."

"Okay." Thad locked the box and placed the key in his pocket. "Now, maybe you can tell us what's happening outside. That's quite a crowd, and most of them don't look too friendly."

"Yes, that's most unfortunate, really. Leon's been a quiet little town for years, outside a drunken cowboy or two on Saturday night. But no problems at all. That's why it was such a shock when some rustlers made off with a small herd of Mr. Larkin's cattle. But the real shock was when the rustlers shot and killed Bobby Sorenson. He was a really nice boy. There was no need for it. Anyway," he waved toward the crowd with his arm, "they're out there wanting to be part of the posse, but I think they'll be more trouble than they're worth. Excuse me."

He picked up the lockbox and headed toward the office. Thad checked his watch and took Beverly's arm.

"I'd say we relax this evening." He turned toward the reception counter as Randal returned. "Where can we find a place to eat?"

"I personally like Zydeco's. It's across the street and three doors down."

******

The owner of Zydeco's was a Cajun who had moved from New Orleans to Leon about three years earlier and rented the empty storefront. He was tight-lipped as to what his plans for the building were, and surprised everyone by turning it into a restaurant.

A pretty woman with unruly black hair and a wild look in her eyes led them to a corner table.

"You're new in town, aren't you?" she said.

"Yes, we just arrived this afternoon."

"Have you eaten Cajun food before?"

"No," Beverly said. "It smells spicy."

"It is, but you'll like it. Of course, my father is the chef, so I grew up with it." The girl handed them two hand-written menus. "Take your time. My name is Yvonne and I'll be back in a minute."

Thad stared at the menu for a few seconds before turning to Beverly.

"So, tell me. I know you took a couple of trips with the old man where I didn't go. Have you ever eaten anything Cajun?"

"No, and there's a lot of French words I should know, but I don't."

"Me neither." Thad looked at the other customer's plate from where he was sitting and laughed. "It looks good."

The waitress returned with a bottle of red wine and a couple of glasses and set them on the table.

"So, have you made up your minds yet?"

"No, and we don't know what to order, so surprise us."

"Okay, how about some blackened cat fish with okra and hush puppies." She popped the wine cork and held it toward Thad to sniff.

"Yes, that smells good."

"Good." She smiled and poured a little in each glass. "I will place your orders with the chef and bring it when it's ready. Let me know if you want anything."

Beverly sipped her wine and grinned. "This is the first taste of wine I've had."

"Really?"

"Yes, Dad says I'm too young."

"Well, yes. I guess he would consider fourteen as too young." Thad toasted her with his glass. "Let's keep it our little secret."

They chatted until the waitress brought their food. "*Bon appetite.*" She grinned and went to seat more guests.

"Well," Thad said, staring at his plate. "I don't know who cooked this, but it looks like he burned the fish."

"She called it *blackened fish,*" Beverly said. "Give it a try before you complain."

Thad took a bite of rice and raised his eyebrows. "A little on the warm side." He then took a bite of the fish and chewed a second or two before grabbing his wine.

"Oh, my god!"

"A little too hot for you, brother?" Beverly laughed.

"Whoa, that *is* hot!"

The waitress came back to their table and placed a hand on Thad's shoulder. "Welcome to New Orleans, sugar. Eat a few more bites before quitting. It gets cooler."

Thad had no way of knowing if the fish really got cooler, or if it was the wine they consumed, but the rough wagon ride from El Dorado to Leon and fighting the huge crowd outside seemed to be a distant memory as they paid their bill.

"I hope you and your wife enjoyed your meals," the waitress said with a warm smile.

Beverly leaned closer to whisper in her ear.

"I know everyone makes the same mistake, but we're not married. He's my brother and he's loaded with money, and he's free game."

They were crossing the street toward the hotel when he asked Beverly what she had said to Yvonne.

"Oh, nothing much. I just told her we were not married, because you were my brother and you are filthy rich."

"No." Thad laughed as he held the door to the hotel open for her. "What did you really tell her?"

"I wouldn't lie to you, Thad. I told her you were rich and single and available."

They climbed the stairs to the second floor.

"What would you say if I started telling everyone you're my rich sister who's looking to get married?"

"Go right ahead. As long as he's handsome and rich, I wouldn't mind getting married. Of course, I think dad would have something to say about me being fourteen." She smiled and kissed his cheek.

"I had a great time this evening. Thanks for taking me there, Thad."

Thad waited until she had closed and locked her door before entering his room and undressing for bed. He fell across his bed and was asleep in minutes.

******

At first Thad thought the pounding on the door was part of his dream. He changed his mind after whoever it was called him an obscene name and tried breaking into the room.

"Hold your horses," Thad yelled and slipped his pants on. He was still buttoning the pants when Beverly opened the adjoining door and poked her head inside.

"Thad? Who is that? What's going on?"

"I don't know." Thad opened the door and was met instantly with a large fist that knocked him to the floor. Beverly screamed and bounced around the room looking for something to throw at the intruders.

"Where is it?" Somebody yelled and hit Thad twice more.

"Ah, come here, darling. I'll make a woman out of you," one of the other men said as he grabbed

Beverly's hair. Instead of pulling away, she charged into him throwing a knee into his groin that bent him over with a loud groan. Then she attacked a second man's face with her fingernails. He bellowed loudly as she kept clawing.

"Alright! Alright!" Harvey Blankenship drug the man off Thad as another man entered carrying a shotgun.

"What's going on in here?" The hotel manager entered the room, then backed away at the sight of Dave's shotgun.

"That's exactly what I'm about to find out." Harvey turned slowly before chuckling. "Okay, come on…. all of you. We're taking this down to the lounge and see if we can't make some sense of it."

******

It took a good fifteen minutes with multiple threats of jail time and confiscation of their horses to get the men to cooperate. The man Beverly had clawed sat moaning and holding a damp bar towel to his wounded face. The one she had kneed was bent over in a chair, looking ill.

"Okay… Randal? We're going to need a bag or a box large enough to collect all their guns and knives, and I want them stored inside your vault. And you need to go home and get a few hours of sleep," he said to Dave Price. "You've got to lead a posse in a few hours. I'll collect all their information and give it to you when you get back."

Harvey waited until Dave was gone before turning toward the big guy who had been beating on the smaller one.

"Now, you tell me your name and what was going on?"

"My name's nobody's business, but we seen 'um checking into their rooms, and they had a big envelope stuffed with money. So, we kind of figured the only way a man could collect that much money was taking up rustling or robbing somebody."

"There's another way," Beverly said.

"And, what way is that?" Harvey shifted in his chair to face her.

"They could have a very wealthy father who sent his son and daughter out here to buy a herd of horses."

"What does he plan on doing with a herd of horses?"

"Sell them to the military. Whether or not you know it, America is at war with Spain, and it looks as though most of Europe might get involved."

"So, your father wants to make a profit out of our war?"

"That's what he does," Thad said as he shifted his weight and groaned. He sees a need and he invests in it."

"And what's your father's name?"

"Thaddeus Jackson the First."

"And is there a second?"

"Yes, I'm Thaddeus Jackson Jr. And I would suggest you call our father on the telephone. There is a stack of business cards and stationery up in my room. I'm fairly sure either him, or his solicitor, will come straighten things out. Also, if Randal will bring our lockbox here, that will answer a lot of questions."

"How's that?" Harvey asked.

"It should prove I came here with the money in the envelope, and didn't steal it after Beverly and I got here."

"Okay," Cotton said as he stood to his feet. "Here's what's going to happen. You two are going back to sleep in your own rooms and hang around town until I get some real answers. And you boys," Cotton pointed toward the men, "are going to sleep in the jail, free of charge."

"Naw, we didn't do nothing outside of roughing him up a little."

"And that's the point, isn't it? Going around, breaking into a man's hotel room and beating the stuffings out of him is against the law. Even a drunken, miserable piece of garbage like you boys ought to know that. Now, let's go, and don't provoke me. This shotgun Dave gave me has a hair trigger."

Cherry Michaels and his friends whined and complained on their way toward jail. Beverly laid a hand against Thad's arm.

"Are you okay?"

"Yeah, sure. At least I think so. Why?"

"That big guy punched you when you opened the door, then punched you several more times."

"Yes, there's that." Thad took Beverly by the arm and escorted her back toward her room. "But the man with all the scratches looked worse. Thanks for defending me."

"My pleasure. Now," Beverly stopped at her door to look at the mess in Thad's room, "the question is, are we going to be able to go back to sleep."

******

The afternoon train from Chicago released a huff of steam as the engineer brought it to a halt. A tall, well-dressed man stepped from one of the cars, followed by two other well-dressed men. Thaddeus Jackson Sr. surveyed the oil field for a couple of minutes before chuckling.

"I realize it's been several years since I've been in El Dorado, but I had no idea a little oil field could change a place so quickly."

"Yes, sir," one of the men said. "What would you like us to do?"

"Well, I'll tell you what I want you to do." Thaddeus paused to watch as some men unloaded a bright red horseless carriage from one of the flat cars. Thaddeus had practiced putting around their Chicago neighborhood after Thaddeus Jr. had taken Beverly west. He found the thing somewhat amusing, although he doubted the practical use of the machine. First of all, one would need to establish refueling stations every thirty to forty miles or so to do any traveling.

"I want Wilcox to come with me, and I want you two to make sure we have all of our luggage, then meet us in Leon tomorrow morning as fast as possible."

Thaddeus Sr. walked toward the horseless carriage as ace attorney Wilcox ran to keep up. "Are you sure the tank is filled?"

"Yes, sir. I saw to it myself."

"Good. If I have calculated correctly, we should arrive in plenty of time to make some sort of statement."

There wouldn't be a next train to Leon until the bridge was repaired, and no one seemed too agreeable to his questions. One thing for certain, even if the bridge was repaired today, the train to Leon wouldn't leave the station until sometime tomorrow, and Thaddeus Sr. was never known for his patience. He decided to take his son's autocar and arrive today.

"Yes, sir. I don't think there's much of a charge against either of your children that I can see. We should have everything wrapped up and be on our way home rather quickly."

"No sir." Thaddeus shook his head. "I didn't get where I am today by quitting. We will make sure the men who attacked my children pay for their crimes, then buy our horses and *then* be on our way home."

Chapter 10

Caroline slipped away shortly after Uncle Harvey promised to use her in his investigation to find Bobby's killer. She mounted Laughing Brook and turned away from the meat market then took the same trail home. No one was at the house when she arrived, so she turned Laughing Brook loose in the corral and washed the red clay from her face. She felt nervous and edgy, so she began doing chores.

First, she collected the eggs and milked the cow, followed by feeding the horses. She had started a fire in the stove and began peeling potatoes by the time the wagon arrived.

"'Wow, I'll stay with mom tending kids every day, if you'll feed the horses," Mark said as Caroline spooned several tablespoons of bacon grease into the hot frying pan.

"Now, why don't I believe that?"

"Because you want me to do it for free?" Mark said with a grin.

"Not hardly." Caroline slid sliced potatoes into the pan and covered them with a lid. "It might be because of the times you promised to do something for me and didn't do it."

"Yeah, there's that… but I meant to do all those things. What can I do to make up for it now?"

Caroline stopped what she was doing and stared at him.

"Are you joking?"

"No, I'm serious. What do you want done right now?"

"How about making biscuits? It would help move things along."

"Okay." Mark rolled up his sleeves.

"Wash your hands first," Caroline said as she turned back to her eggs. "You want two or three eggs?"

"Three, of course. What else do you want me to do?"

Vicky stood outside in the dark and motioned for Matthew to be quiet as he came onto the front porch. He crept up on the porch and leaned his head next to hers.

"Just watch," Vicky whispered in his ear. Matthew watched for a couple of minutes as Mark made a pan of drop biscuits and set the pan on the edge of the stove, ready to put in the Dutch oven.

"Lord have mercy," Matthew said and scooped Rose into his arms as she darted by. "God is well and miracles still happen."

"Oh, hi, Dad," Caroline said as she turned the potatoes. "I thought you'd be out with the posse."

"I am. I needed to pick up a couple of things before we get any farther away."

"And, of course, a good hot meal wouldn't hurt you either," Mark said with a laugh.

"I've never denied loving to eat. And if the rest of them forgot to bring something warm to eat..." He shrugged. "That's their fault, not mine."

Vicky took Rose from Matthew's arms and wiped her face and hands with a damp hand towel.

"What kind of a posse did you find yourself leading?"

"Mmm, I could use a few less people, but not too bad."

"How long before they start dropping out?" Caroline asked as she stirred and re-covered the potatoes in the pan.

"I expect there will be two or three dropping out in the morning. It depends on who's used to sleeping on the ground." Matthew grabbed a coffee mug from the cabinet. "Is the coffee about done?"

"It should be," Caroline said as Mark put the biscuits in the oven. "Grab your plates and forks."

There was a shuffling of chairs and a clinking of dishes as Caroline tossed bacon into a pan and broke several eggs. They held hands as Matthew prayed, asking for God's blessings on their home, and safety for the posse.

"So, who would you rather have on your posse?" Caroline asked as she scooted up to the table.

"You, of course." Matthew grinned and buttered a biscuit.

"Is that all… the two of us?"

"It doesn't take a lot." Matthew laid the knife aside and took a bite. "I'd like Dave. It's always nice to have some law handy. Then, Benjamin Polk. He sees things most people would miss. And, Jack Caldwell. That would make a pretty good posse."

"Well," Vicky spooned a bite of scrambled eggs into Rose's mouth. "Regardless of who's on your posse, I want you back safe and sound, Matthew Blue."

"The feeling is mutual, my dear." He stuffed a piece of bacon into a biscuit and took a bite. "I hate leaving you and the kids out here by yourselves."

"We hate it when you have to leave, even for a day or two." Vicky leaned across the table to give him a kiss.

******

Matthew lay on his back and watched her when she first arrived. There was no denying who the lone figure was, since the pony moved as silently as she did. Most people will make some noise, even the snapping of a tiny twig or the scurrying of a rodent. Matthew smiled and closed his eyes. Caroline was just like her mother in many ways. Overly kind and giving to a fault, but with a strong sense of justice. She would never admit to joining the posse for even one minute, and when the sun rose in the morning there wouldn't be any evidence of her having been there.

Chapter 11

Thaddeus Jackson Sr. rose early in spite of having spent half the night sitting in Harvey Blankenship's living room, discussing the trouble Thaddeus Jr. and Beverly had had with the men at the hotel.

"I take it the boy didn't try to defend himself?" Thaddeus said.

"When I came into the room, the boy was trying to defend hisself the best he could, while being held down by one fellow and getting punched in the face by another." Harvey refilled their cups.

"Oh, that's good to hear." Thaddeus gave a crooked grin. "He was on the boxing team in college, but I've been a little worried about that. I've never seen him defend himself… ever. He's always had things handed to him." Thaddeus sipped his coffee. "Do you have children, Mr. Blankenship?"

"No, Alice and I've been trying for close to thirty years, but no luck. We wanted to have a passel of grandkids by now, but I'm afraid we're past the child-rearing time of our lives. Those two of yours seem like fine young folks."

"Oh, they are. I'm sure I don't tell them enough, but I always wanted them to be tough and able to take care of themselves."

"Well, one thing I learned out of being a lawman for close to thirty years is that some of the toughest people out there never touch a gun or punch someone in the face. But they're pure hell running a business, and you never want to cross them.

"Amen to that." Thaddeus checked his pocket watch. "I guess I had better go wake Thad and Beverly. I have no idea what he'll be able to do, let alone eat, this morning."

******

Doctor Jonathan Williams rapped on the hotel door and received no answer. He had been assured by the man at the reception desk that neither of the guests had come from their rooms. He was about to try one more time when the door swung open and Beverly poked her head out.

"I'm sorry, but my brother isn't feeling well. May I help you?"

"Yes, I'm what people consider to be a doctor in this God-forsaken town. Sheriff Blankenship asked me to check on Thaddeus' condition."

"Oh, please come in." Beverly stepped back to let Dr. Williams inside. Thaddeus was sitting on the edge of the bed holding a damp washcloth over his mouth. The doctor set his medical bag on the bed and opened it.

"Yeah, they sure did a number on you, didn't they? I'm going to need you to lay crossways across the bed, so we can get as much light as possible. He jerked the drapes open wide.

He glanced at Beverly for a few seconds.

"I may need to enlist your aid. Are you up to it?"

"Sure." Beverly nodded as Thaddeus started laughing, then covered his mouth with an "Oh, that hurts."

"It's good to see you can still laugh. What did you find so funny?"

"Our home actually sits in the country, outside of Chicago. One of Beverly's favorite things to do was to go kill and field-dress a deer before going to school."

"Oh," Dr. Williams said with a chuckle. "I guess you're up to helping me patch you brother back together. I also treated a drunken man inside the jail this morning that looked like he'd gotten into a fight with an alley-cat and lost. I reckon that was your handywork?"

"I would have scratched his eyes out if I could have reached them." Beverly answered the door as someone rapped loudly on it.

"Good morning, Dad." She swung the door open. "Come in. The doctor's about to look in Thad's mouth."

"I will, unless someone else interrupts us. Now, lay back and open your mouth really wide."

Doctor Williams leaned over him. "Hmm. Bring the lamp closer."

"What about the man who got beaten up by the alley-cat?" Beverly asked.

"Ah, yes. Besides being nearly clawed to death, he was also one of the dirtiest men I've ever seen. So, I'm thinking your brother might heal quicker than that man."

Beverly held the desk lamp as the doctor completed his examination.

"You may sit up now." He patted Thad on the shoulder.

"Well, I'm starving to death," Beverly said. "What can he eat?"

"Oh, they pretty well shredded the inside of his mouth. So, it will be a matter of what he can stand to eat. I'd recommend staying away from anything spicy for a few days. But the most important part is keeping your mouth clean, so after every meal, rinse your mouth with salty water."

"Ow!" Beverly cringed. "That's gonna hurt, Doc."

"Yes, and he'll hate me for a while, but that's better than letting it get infected. Okay," he patted Thad once more. "My office is about a block and a half west of here, so come and see me if you have any problems."

******

Thaddeus Jackson strolled down the crowded plank walkway with his two children. About half of the people they met stepped off the walkway to make room for them, although Thaddeus never asked them to, or even gave the slightest hint he wished them to.

"Maybe it's because you asked us to wear the best clothing we brought," Thad said.

"Yes, I did ask, but I didn't realize you were bringing your best business suit. I thought you and Beverly were bringing something more appropriate to the west."

"And how were we supposed to know what that was? Neither of us had ever seen the wild west."

"Yes, I suppose you're right. Now, we'll have to go someplace to show it off."

"What the…" Thad said as they approached a small crowd in front of Beth's Café.

"Oh yes, I forgot to tell you I had the railroad ship your horseless carriage to you."

"Well, thank you, Dad. But why?"

"Both you and Beverly told me over the telephone that, for some reason, the horses in Kansas had all disappeared. So, I thought we might need some form of transportation while we're here."

The small crowd parted as Cotton stopped to stare at the autocar. "It sure is shiny."

"Yes," Thaddeus said with a chuckle. "The people who assembled the darned thing said to keep it that way and it will keep its value."

"Now, that'd be a neat trick." Cotton shook his head. "It'd be the first time someone bought something that grew in value after you paid for it. Let me know how that works out."

"Yes, I will," Thaddeus raised his voice as Cotton ambled down the sidewalk.

"I don't know about the rest of you, but I'm still starving," Beverly said as she reached for the café door and it seemed to open on its own account.

"Oh," Beverly said, clutching her breast. "Mr. Wilcox. I didn't know you were here."

"Your father wanted a law team to be here in case there were some charges filed against you two. Everyone can relax now, because the only charges filed are against the men who assaulted you inside your hotel rooms."

"That's good news, Wilcox. When is the hearing going to happen?" Thaddeus held the door open for everyone.

"Actually," Wilcox chuckled, "the judge is a fellow named Silas Wilson, who also raises hogs. He's got a shipment of hogs ready to ship. He told me once his hogs are shipped, he'll conduct a hearing on your case. The only trouble is, with the bridge out, no telling when that might be."

They all sat and the waitress slid a pot of coffee and some cups onto their table.

"And so, the judge has no idea when the hearing might take place?"

"Not a clue."

"So, we might as well enjoy ourselves while we're here." Thaddeus Sr. nodded.

******

Beverly ordered a plate of pancakes with sausage, bacon and two eggs covered with syrup. She had only taken two bites before feeling guilty seeing her brother struggle to eat gravy over biscuits, especially when it looked like he was only able to consume about half the serving. The really painful part of breakfast was when Thaddeus Jr. had to rinse out his mouth, and finished by being hunched over a washbasin with his body trembling.

Beverly went to the veranda off her bedroom and cried.

Chapter 12

Matthew grinned as he opened his saddle bag and discovered a deerskin necklace woven together with multi-colored beads that belonged to Caroline. He had no idea when she slipped it inside the bag, only that it was her way of wishing love and safety over him and the entire posse. The posse had lost its steam after being in the field only two days. They lost four members the first day who said they had to take care of their families, then lost three more the following day, leaving a posse of half-hearted men. Matthew and Dave decided to disband the posse and return home. Then, a day later, Matthew would leave with a smaller posse of hand-picked men.

Leaving the saddlebag on the porch, Matthew returned to the corral and unsaddled the pinto then turned him loose inside the corral to roll and work the kinks out. He loosened the pack on the pack horse then stopped as an unfamiliar "pock-pock-pock" sound reached his ears, mingled with the laughter of a young woman. Matthew dropped the pack that had been on the pack horse and turned the animal loose inside the corral as a shiny red horseless carriage appeared on the road from behind some brush and a few seconds later rolled to a stop in front of Matthew. The pretty teenaged girl who was driving was the same one who had everyone sign her book at the depot. She flashed him a brilliant smile and turned off the engine.

Matthew walked slowly around the autocar and stopped near the left front wheel. The wheels were made of wood and the vehicle had brass letters across the front spelling *Duryea*. A tall, husky man stood and offered Matthew his hand.

"I'm Thaddeus Jackson, and these two young people are my children. I do hope you will forgive the intrusion, Mr. Blue, but I hope to borrow a few minutes of your time to discuss some business. I would have telephoned, but it seems that you don't have one."

"I suppose so. My wife and children are on their way home from school now, but should be home in an hour or so. You might want to park this thing over near to the pond. I'd hate to see Vicky hit it while turning the buckboard around. Right now, you're parked exactly where she loves to park."

The young man climbed from the back of the vehicle and took the crank from his sister's hand.

"I can crank it, Thad."

"I know you can, but the motor is hot, and if it backfires, it could break your arm. You sit in the driver's seat and start the engine when it catches."

"Quit treating me like a… "

"Sister?" Matthew cocked his head to one side. "Actually, the boy's right. I had to make a trip to El Dorado a few weeks ago and I saw George Bennett, owner of the mercantile, get his arm broken when the horseless carriage he was trying to crank kicked back with a loud bang. The way he fell, I thought someone shot him at first. But it gave him a compound fracture. There was a hunk of bone poking up right here." He pointed toward his right arm. "But you go right ahead and do what you think you should do."

Matthew stepped back to watch the show but the motor started on the second turn of the crank. Thaddeus climbed into the forward passenger seat and pointed to a flat area near the pond then Beverly guided the vehicle around the chicken coop.

"She handles that thing pretty well," Matthew said.

"I had to get a couple of pillows for her to sit on, but yes, she does a lot better than me," Thaddeus said with a chuckle. "I drove it fairly well on some paved, level streets in Chicago. But out here, where nothing's level or paved, I don't do so well. Have you ridden in one of them, Mr. Blue?"

"Not hardly. I've watched people fool around in them in El Dorado and the last time I was in Chicago. But I'd rather fork one of my horses and cut across the land. I think I'd get there quicker, and I wouldn't have to worry about running out of fuel or breaking down."

Thad laughed again as the young people joined them. "I think you might be right, Mr. Blue."

Matthew studied Thaddeus' son for a few seconds before shaking his head.

"I see you didn't follow my advice, did you?"

"I didn't have time. But this had nothing to do with my name."

"Wait a minute. Have you two already met? Why didn't you tell me?"

"We met for just a few minutes at the train depot in El Dorado. But the place was swamped with people coming and going, and Mr. Blue was in a hurry and I didn't know he raised horses."

"What advice did you give my son?"

"Nothing much." Matthew licked the cigarette he had finished rolling.

"Mr. Blue told Thad to change his name and how he dresses," Beverly said.

"Well, I didn't say a word about the way you talk, but that sounds pretty close to what I told you," Matthew said.

"Why didn't you listen to him?"

"Because I had four thugs break into my hotel room and beat the stuffing out of me."

"Outside of you getting the stuffing kicked out of you, it doesn't matter much one way or the other," Matthew said as he lit the cigarette. "Come on, let's go to the house and get a cup of coffee."

******

Matthew leaned against the doorpost sipping the dregs in the bottom of his mug. The buckboard coming toward him seemed to disappear as it dropped into a wash then reappeared a few seconds later. There was a rider on horseback following them.

"They're here," he said, tossing the remnants of the mug into the yard, making several chickens scatter. "I don't know how you girls got loose, but you need to get back into the pen."

He stepped off the porch as Vicky guided the horses in a wide circle that swung the buckboard around to face the opposite direction, ready to load the children and homework assignments for the next school day.

"Amazing," Thaddeus said as he joined Matthew's side.

"What's amazing?"

"Your wife, for one thing. Not only is she very pretty, but she parked the wagon exactly as you said she would."

Matthew cocked his head to one side and raised his eyebrows thoughtfully as Thaddeus removed his derby and offered an assisting hand for Vicky as she climbed out of the wagon.

Jack Caldwell was the horseman following the buckboard. He dismounted at the corral, then he walked toward them, staring at the people piling out of the buckboard.

"Thank you, sir. I don't believe we've met. I'm Vicky Blue, and, you are?"

"I'm Thaddeus Jackson the First. My son, who is standing by your husband, is Thaddeus Jackson Jr."

Vicky grabbed Rose and a basket full of books from the buckboard and paused at the door long enough to kiss Matthew on the lips.

"Here, take your daughter. I'm sorry for being a little late, but one of my students needed help with this week's homework assignment, like she does every day."

"That's quite alright. We kept ourselves entertained." Matthew turned toward Caroline and Mark who were busy getting acquainted with Thad Jr. and Beverly.

"Alright, let's get the chores done while we have daylight."

Jack Caldwell and Thad Jr. both fell in step with Caroline as she began mucking out the stalls. Beverly Jackson collected eggs while Mark chased the two wayward chickens back into the pen.

"Now, that's something I never expected to see anytime soon," Thaddeus said as he helped himself to another mug of coffee.

"And what's that, Mr. Jackson?" Vicky asked.

"My children offering to help. I'm afraid they've always paid someone to do their chores for them."

"Really?" Vicky laughed. "And what does your wife have to say about that?"

"My wife passed away while giving birth to Beverly. But I'm positive that she would like who they've turned out to be… except for being slightly on the lazy side."

"There could be worse things," Matthew said. "From what I've seen, they're polite and well mannered. Except for Beverly trying to scratch that drunken sidewinder's eyes out, and that was because they broke into the hotel to give the boy a pretty good beating. I don't blame her."

"Oh, I don't either. I'm happy they stand up for each other. I just want them to become useful."

"I think they will be. Just enjoy them while you can. In the meantime," Matthew stretched, "you can help me figure out where everyone's going to sleep."

"Oh, don't worry about us. We have rooms at the hotel in town."

"And I'm sure they are neat and clean." Vicky lit another kerosene burner on the stove. "But it's almost ten miles into Leon, and the road has several dips and curves that are pretty hazardous at night. and If I'm not mistaken it will get dark well before you reach town."

"So, I'd recommend a nice pallet over here." Matthew stomped his foot on the floor. It stays fairly warm from the stove, and Tippy the dog will keep you company."

******

Matthew went to the root cellar and fetched a ham and a panful of potatoes. Then he stood by the door directing traffic as the young people finished their chores and came to the house.

"Hang on there. You all are going to be eating our vittles, so you can cook them first."

"I don't know how to cook," Beverly said as she smiled at Matthew.

"That's okay, you'll learn." Matthew stopped Jack Caldwell and pointed him in the direction of the table.

"You know how to make biscuits. I've seen you do it, and I ate one of them. They weren't half-bad, so you teach this young lady how."

"What? Make biscuits?"

"That's what we're talking about."

Vicky sat at the table, feeding Rose a scrambled egg and a glass of warm milk. For dessert, she buttered a biscuit and smeared a thin layer of homemade blue berry jam on it. She slid her chair up to the table as Caroline set a plate piled high with fried potatoes, ham and scrambled eggs in front of her.

"Vicky? Would you please say the blessing?" Matthew asked.

Rose fell asleep halfway through the meal, so Matthew took her and allowed his wife to eat.

"Ah, Mr. Blue?" Jack Caldwell said with a swallow.

"Yes?"

"Sheriff Price said for you to contact him right away."

"He wants to deputize another posse?"

"Yes sir."

"It figures. I knew he'd be chomping at the bit, so I already have the list stuffed in my jacket pocket. I'll give it to you in the morning."

"I suppose I'm not a member?" Caroline said.

"No, you're not. I talked to both Cotton and Dave and they say no."

"And what do you say?"

Matthew pursed his lips and looked at the ceiling before turning back toward Caroline.

"I say no, but for a different reason."

"And what's that?"

"Your mother needs you."

"Aw! She has Mark. Besides, I can ride a horse better than most men, and I can shoot better."

"Maybe you can, but we spent a small fortune sending you to that school to be certified as a teacher, then to finishing school. And I'd hate to lose my investment." He stopped to laugh. "And, if you throw that biscuit in your hand, I'll turn you over my knee and paddle your backside."

Chapter 13

Fifteen-year-old Mary Turner's lace-up high-top shoes made a dull thunking noise as she strolled down the plank walkway from the library toward the hotel. The right shoe's thunk was deeper than the left's, which meant the leather tab on the heel was completely gone and the wooden right heel was digging into the walkway. A few more days of wood against wood would likely cause the heel to give away and the shoe would have to be repaired or thrown away.

She paused as she turned to cross the street to deliver a clean and pressed shirt to her brother at the hotel. A group of men were congregated on the walkway and talking. One of them looked like the nice man who ran the meat market. He smiled at her and returned to talking. Mary's right heel caught on a loose board as she stepped from the walkway to the street, twisting her ankle. She pulled back as the board flipped up, but that caused her to fall backwards and only made it worse as the board slammed shut, holding her foot like a vise.

Mary released a whimper as her brother's shirt she was carrying slipped from her hand to the steps.

A strong arm wrapped around her waist, holding her up. "Here, let me help you. Put your arm around my neck. Well, go on," he added as she hesitated. "I don't bite."

Mary looked up to find she was only inches from Andrew's smiling face as he reached down and unhooked her foot.

"Okay, now I've got you, so sit on my arm. Come on," he added when she hesitated a second time. "I won't drop you."

Mary relaxed as Andrew carried her to a bench near the door of the pharmacy and gently placed her on it.

"Now let's see how much damage that loose board caused."

"Thank you, Mr. Turner, but I think I can make it by myself."

Mary tried standing but fell back onto the bench with another whimper when her foot touched the sidewalk.

"I don't think you're going anywhere with your ankle twisted up like that," Andrew said with a crooked grin. "The question is, how bad did you hurt your ankle?"

Sheriff Price jogged across the street. "What's going on, Andrew?"

"Um, Miss Mary started to cross the street when that loose board in the steps here," Andrew pointed, "popped open and twisted her ankle."

"Henry!" Dave Price bellowed. "Stop what you're doing and get yourself out here. Now!"

Everyone took a couple of steps back as Henry Adams came to the door.

"What's got your goat, Dave? I'm in the middle of inventory."

"Forget inventory. I'm in the middle of trying to save your ornery butt from being sued. I thought I told you awhile back to get that step fixed."

"Yeah, you did and I drove a couple of nails in it."

"Well, whatever you did didn't work." Dave picked up the loose board and flipped it over. There were several nails that had completely missed the board they were intended to be nailed to. "Well, that ain't gonna work, Henry."

"How was I supposed to know? It looked tight to me."

"Don't you check when you finish a job to make sure it's okay?"

"Sometimes… yeah, but not always."

"Lord have mercy," Andrew said with a laugh. "Remind me to buy all my aspirin at some other store."

"I need a couple of men to go behind my office and bring back some sawhorses to block these steps," Dave said. "I'll need a hammer and some sixteen-penny nails from you, Henry."

"I don't rightly know if I still have those around.

"You'd better take a look and find out."

"Okay, okay. Calm down. I'll take a look-see."

"I am calm, Henry. It's you who needs to be reminded this building needs to be safe, and right now it isn't, so your pharmacy is closed 'til further notice."

"Aw, come on, Dave. Give a guy a break."

"You're still closed. Get me the hammer and nails."

Andrew knelt in front of Mary and raised the hem of her dress a couple of inches and told her to hold it there.

"What are you doing, Mr. Thomas?"

"I am going to remove you shoe so we can see if you need to see the doctor."

"Here's Randal's shirt, Mary." Dave Price laid the slightly smudged white shirt over the back of the bench. "I think it might be good enough for tonight."

"Thank you, Sheriff Price."

She gripped the bench and winced as Andrew worked her shoe off her foot and pulled her sock off. The ankle was already swelling and turning black and blue.

"What do you think, Sheriff? Take her to the doctor?"

Dave pursed his lips and nodded. It might not be broken, but I'd feel better if Doc Williams said so." With that, Andrew dropped her shoe and Randy's shirt into her lap and scooped her off the bench.

"Whoa, hold on there, Andy. I'm sure Henry's got a wheelchair of sorts inside the store."

Andrew laughed as the spectators made room for him to cross the street.

"She isn't very heavy, Sheriff. Certainly not as heavy as lifting and wrapping a full-grown beef."

******

Dr. Williams said Mary's ankle wasn't broken, but ordered her to take a few days off work and to get plenty of rest. Andrew carried her home and explained to her mother what had taken place, making it sound a little worse than what had actually happened.

Andrew checked his pocket watch and leaned to give Mary a quick hug. "I've got to get some work done, but I'll check back after I close the shop to see how you're doing. And don't bother with supper. I'll bring it with me."

He then returned home and checked the ice level in the cool room and found it dangerously low with maybe two or three days left, before he had to start throwing meat away. He chose four prime steaks and took them to Zydeco's and asked Yvonne to do something special with them including side dishes, and he would pick the order up around 5:30.

Andrew then poked his head into Henry's pharmacy and gave him an update on Mary Turner's condition.

"Well, you can tell her for me I'm sorry that she got hurt here at my store, and she can use these until she heals." He handed Andrew a pair of crutches.

******

Mary Turner sat on the front porch listening to her mother as she expounded the glowing virtues of her husband and Mary had to fight to keep from screaming *that's not true, Mother*. After a few moments Mrs. Turner excused herself and Andrew joined Mary on the front porch.

"I'm sorry about that," she said as he sat beside her.

"You're sorry about what?"

"About her lying to you about my father. He was…"

"Shhh," he said holding a finger against her lips. "I've lived in this town long enough to hear all the good and the bad concerning the people who live here. Let's talk about something pleasant."

Mary laughed. "You heard what my father's like and you chose to sit on the porch with me?"

"Why not? I haven't heard anyone say you're lying in the street drunk." They both laughed, then talked awhile longer before Andrew checked his pocket watch and said he had to leave.

"I'll check on you tomorrow." He leaned to kiss her forehead and she grabbed him around the neck and planted a kiss on his lips. Then, she released him with an "Oh, my gosh, I'm sorry," and began a litany of excuses for the kiss. Andrew leaned forward and covered her lips with his.

"That should give you something to think about while I'm working tomorrow."

Mary watched Andrew until he completely disappeared between the buildings, then put herself to bed. *Thank you, Jesus.* Andrew Thomas liked her.

Chapter 14

A cool breeze entered when Matthew came up from the root cellar carrying two coffee mugs. "Here." He handed one mug to Thaddeus Sr. "It's got something a little extra in it."

Thaddeus sipped it and nodded appreciatively.

"Tennessee sour mash, if I'm not mistaken. I'm impressed. How'd you get it way out here?"

"It's a matter of working for the sheriff every now and then. Kansas is a dry state, so when a whisky peddler tried to smuggle a bunch of it into Leon, we caught and fined him, then sent him back where he came from. Then, since this is a dry state, we had to dispose of the whisky.

"I take it not all of it was disposed of," Thaddeus said before taking another sip.

"There's disposing, and there's disposing." Matthew lifted his mug.

"You said you wanted to discuss a business proposition with me. What type of business?"

"Horses, Mr. Blue. I want to buy as many horses as I can lay my hands on."

Matthew raised his eyebrows and took a sip from his coffee mug.

"That sounds interesting. May I ask what you plan on doing with the horses?"

"Hang on to them until the time is right, and sell them to The United States military."

"Ah, now I see. You must be expecting our country to go to war in the near future. Aren't you risking me simply bypassing you and selling my horses directly to the military?"

"No." Thaddeus chuckled. "I've already signed a contract with the Department of Defense and I already have a place to keep them stored until they want them. Do you think we can work out a deal, Mr. Blue?"

"It's possible. But most of my horses are broke, and have some training as working horses. They might be too expensive for what you want. But we'll see tomorrow morning. I'll show you what we have and you can quote me a price."

******

Thaddeus Sr. woke at the crack of dawn with a stiff neck that sent a screaming pain into his shoulder when he moved. When he finally rolled over to his hands and knees, Caroline's dog, Tippy, growled at him.

"Oh, go growl at yourself." He struggled to reach the edge of the table and clung to it for dear life until he got his bearings. There was a lantern shining inside the barn and, if he remembered correctly, the outhouse was at the rear of the barn. Thaddeus pulled himself upward as he staggered to his feet. It was a chore just getting to the front door, and finding the latch in the dark was another mountain to climb. Thaddeus believed he'd won that battle as the door swung open and Tippy shot past him to hike his leg against the hitching post.

He walked hunched-over to the outhouse and had to fight the dog who had decided it was time to play. His body was feeling somewhat normal as he passed the barn on his way back to the house. Matthew was busy braiding and waxing a long string of leather. Thaddeus couldn't help himself and stepped inside.

"And what, may I ask, are you doing now?"

Matthew looked up, then went back to his braiding.

"Caroline gave me an English longbow when she got home. She got it from a professor who was retiring. I noticed the bowstring was frayed, so I'm making a new one."

"When can we go look at your horses, Mr. Blue?"

"That depends a lot on Dave Price's posse." Matthew drew the bowstring across the work bench and locked a wooden arm, holding the string tight.

"Since there was a murder involved, they're hoping to catch these rustlers as soon as possible."

"Hmm," Thaddeus said thoughtfully. "You could have fooled me. This is what, four days since they committed the crime?"

"No," Matthew said as he washed his hands. "It's actually been three days, and tomorrow is the funeral. We did have a posse out there part of the time." Matthew tossed the pan of water into the yard and dried his hands. "It's a little later than I'd like to get a posse moving." He hung the towel on a wooden peg. "But not bad. If we hurry, I can show you one of the remudas right after coffee."

******

The corral was set behind a row of trees and brush about a hundred yards from the Blue ranch house. Thaddeus had to chuckle to himself that Matthew and Vicky Blue knew exactly how to build a thriving business. Anything to do with horses and cattle, like the large barn and the extra-large corral with feeding troughs, were necessary items... like air. The fancy house, opposed to the log cabin they were living in now, would come once the finances were established.

"What I don't understand is, I spent a good part of yesterday afternoon at your house, not a hundred yards away, and didn't see this corral," Thaddeus said, looking back the way they'd come.

"You're not supposed to see this corral. If you could see it, then I did a lousy job of building it."

A big, glossy black stallion trotted over to say hello.

"This is midnight," Matthew said as he cut an apple in two and fed half of it to the horse. "My son named him."

"These horses are better than I expected, Mr. Blue. How many more can you get me?"

"How many do want?"

"A hundred head... maybe more if I can get them."

"Let me do a count on how many I have on the ranch. That'll give us a starting point. Then we can get more from Jim Larkin. His horses are good. And if you want more, I can talk to White Cloud."

"Sounds Indian," Thaddeus said with a chuckle.

"He is. Comanche. Matthew gave the second half of the apple to Midnight.

"Now, I've got to get to Leon and see about my posse."

Chapter 15

Caroline cringed as Frieda Wilson hit a sour note of *All Hail the Power of Jesus' Name* on the organ and followed it with three more.

I'm sorry, Bobby. I tried to tell everyone years ago that there wasn't anything wrong with the old organ the church had. They needed to get someone who could play it.

Sunday mornings were a real treat, Caroline thought. Frieda got the chance to slaughter three, sometimes four, Gospel hymns, one after another. What Caroline could not understand was why no one said or did anything in all the years Frieda sat on the bench facing the organ. Someone told her that Frieda, at one time, was a good organ player, but Caroline had never witnessed any of that.

She braced herself as Frieda Wilson made the organ screech and howl its way through a solo of *Sweet Hour of Prayer.*

She allowed her eyes to drift to the left where Albert Meeks was seated with his wife and daughter. In a matter of a month or so, she would bear him another baby. Albert claimed it didn't matter to him if it was a boy or girl as long as it was healthy, but Caroline suspected he was sort of twisting the truth some. Every man she knew wanted a son.

She allowed her eyes to drift to the right where Thaddeus Jackson was seated with his two children. It was nice of them to attend Bobby's funeral. Alice Blankenship told her that Thaddeus had paid for the extremely large spray of flowers near the coffin. No one would have thought badly of them if they hadn't shown up, especially since they didn't know Bobby or anyone in town.

Well, that wasn't exactly true, since Mr. Jackson chose to have his daughter, Beverly, drive his family in his son's autocar to Caroline's parent's ranch in an attempt to buy horses. At first, the move angered her since she had already made up her mind she certainly did not like Thaddeus Jr., not even in the least bit. In her opinion, he was arrogant and condescending. Of course, the man was far better educated than most people.

But that was all before those men broke into Thad's hotel room and beat him half to death. At first, she thought the beating was payback for a bad business deal Thad had made, until Matthew told her the truth. Then the winds of sympathy shifted slightly toward Thad. Now, she found herself actually liking the man. And there was Beverly to consider. She found the girl amusing and head-strong and willing to fight to her own death defending her brother. She proved that by attacking the man with her fingernails to save Thaddeus. In short, Caroline believed that she and Beverly Jackson could become good friends.

The howling of the organ caused Caroline to jerk in the pew. Pastor Billings was just finishing his sermon on the resurrection of Lazarus. She shifted in an effort to get more comfortable under the weight of her petticoats. She was positive those who designed the latest in modern fashion were somehow working with American politics to keep females subservient to men, and miserable. One of the first things she was going to do once Bobby Sorenson was laid to rest was to change into something more comfortable.

The pall bearers took their place as the audience passed by the coffin and stood in honor outside the door. Sweat trickled between Caroline's shoulder blades as the coffin was loaded into the old, white horse-drawn hearse. She swallowed hard as the hearse reached the graveside and stopped. A flood of memories swept through her mind. Bobby Sorenson had been one of her best friends since they were small children. He was the one who taught her how to make and use a slingshot. She in turn taught him how to gig frogs. He stood up for her when she dressed like a Comanche warrior before running onto the baseball diamond.

She swallowed again as the pall bearers hoisted the coffin from the hearse and set it over the open grave. A sob escaped her lips as they lowered the coffin into the ground. It suddenly dawned on her that she would never see her friend again… ever. Her body shook with each sob. Somebody handed her a handkerchief and patted her back. Not being able to see who her benefactor was, Caroline held the handkerchief to her eyes and leaned against whoever it was until the sobbing stopped.

Caroline took a step back and blew her nose. Thad Jr. nodded at her with a slight smile and turned his attention back toward Pastor Billings as he said the benediction.

Caroline stood quietly, listening to the prayer for a couple of minutes before she realized Thad still had his arm around her shoulders. She quietly removed his hand and whispered a small thank you.

******

They were at the post funeral luncheon when things seemed to go from bad to worse in a hurry. Thad was picking his way through the picnic tables set in front of the church building, holding a plate of fried chicken, mashed potatoes and an ear of fresh-picked corn, with a cup of lemonade in his other hand. He had made sure Caroline Blue was seated safely beside her mother before waiting in line at the tables where the food was being served. He never would have been so bold as to touch her, especially after hearing that she was engaged to one of John Larkin's cowboys. His only excuse was that she looked as though she were going to pass out. So, he had rushed to her side, offering a clean handkerchief and a comforting shoulder to lean on. It wasn't until later that he discovered through Beverly that they'd drawn quite a bit of attention.

"No, I might tease you about some things, Thad, but I'd never tease you about something like this. I like her, and I hope you ask her to marry you. But just so you'll know, you evidently ruffled her boyfriend's feathers, and he might want to fight."

"Well, first of all, I didn't know she was really spoken for until a few minutes ago, and second, I don't think anyone would want to start a fight at their best friend's funeral."

"I wouldn't be so sure of that. He's got to save face somehow."

Thad had just reached Caroline's table when someone called his name. He turned to see who it was and was met with a fist that knocked him onto the table, which collapsed to the ground. Several women screamed as the table fell, knocking cups of lemonade and hot coffee, and scattering plates of food.

"Oh, God, what is wrong with this town?" Thad yelled as he tried to get to his feet while brushing mashed potatoes and gravy off his vest and trying to avoid getting hit again.

"What are you doing, Jack Caldwell?" Thad looked up to see Caroline brushing food from her dress. Caldwell was doing a weird little dance while holding his clenched fists in the air.

"You stay out of this, Caroline. I'm defending your honor."

"You're what?" Caroline almost screamed the words, making Jack back several feet away.

Mary Turner was standing next to Andrew Thomas and burst into a fit of laughter as several men and women scrambled to clean up the mess.

"My honor has never been in question and doesn't need to be defended. Just look at this dress! I knew I should have changed. Look at Thad's clothes. Do you have any idea how long it takes to wash and iron this dress? No, don't touch me!" she added as Jack reached for her.

"Okay, okay, break it up. What's going on here?" Harvey Blankenship said as he elbowed his way through the crowd.

"For some reason, Jack Caldwell thinks my honor needs to be defended, so he punched Mr. Jackson in the face."

"Is that right, Jack?"

"Well, yeah… but he was making advances toward her when they were burying Bobby Sorenson, and he had his arm around her shoulders… right there in front of everyone."

"You're nuts!" Thad yelled and then added a "thank you" to a woman who handed him a towel.

"All Mr. Jackson was doing was comforting me. Bobby's death had fully hit me at that time and I couldn't stop crying." Caroline took several steps to yell at Jack.

"Which *you* would have known, if you weren't watching Beverly so closely." She spun on her heel and brushed at her dress angrily.

"Bu… but… Caroline…"

Thad started for the hotel room to change his clothes but stopped to eye Jack Caldwell. "Oh, by the way. The reason we came to Leon was to buy horses—a *lot* of horses. Just so you'll know, we won't be buying any horses from the ranch you work at."

"It appears you have yourself a real problem." Jack looked up to see his boss, James Larkin, unwrapping a cigar.

"You'll have to go get that account back, or find yourself a different job."

"How do I do that?"

"That's *your* problem to fix. Promise them anything, but get them to buy some of our horses. If not, you'll have to clear out."

Three dogs scampered about under the table feasting on the chicken and mashed potatoes before two of them got into a disagreement over a drumstick.

"Hey, knock it off… now!" Harvey Blankenship yelled as he tossed a different piece of chicken into a clump of brush. The two dogs charged the brush with growls and snarls, leaving several pieces for the third dog who was eating quietly under the table.

"Ladies?" Thaddeus Jackson said with a warm smile. "I am terribly sorry that my son was involved in this whole affair."

"Oh, your son didn't do a thing wrong," Vicky said and turned toward her daughter. "What do you think, Caroline? Did Thad do anything wrong?"

"No, but Jack certainly did. He has no idea what this dress cost me waiting on tables. Now, look at it. It's ruined. Simply ruined."

"Oh, I don't know," Thaddeus said. "A good dry cleaner might be able to do something with it. In the meantime, why don't you ladies follow Beverly to the mercantile and see if there isn't something you'd be willing to wear the rest of the day. It's my way of saying we're sorry."

"Well, what are you waiting on?" Beverly said as she noticed her father escorting Yvonne toward her restaurant. "We have a lot of shopping to do."

"Actually, Caroline's dress is worse than mine, so you take her. I'll wait here" Vicky said.

"No, no, no," Beverly said tend grabbed Vicky's arm. "Dad's given us the go-ahead, so you're going too."

"Yes, but buying clothes at the mercantile is expensive. You'd better get his okay before we actually buy anything," Vicky said as she pulled back. Beverly started laughing as she looked Vicky and Caroline in the eyes.

"You don't have any idea how much money my daddy has, do you?" She tugged on their arms, dragging them along. "Well, you know what? Neither does he. Working hard and making money is like a game to him. So, let's go see what they have. I haven't been in a store like this in years. It'll be fun."

******

Thad Jr. had to pass the jail in order to reach the hotel.

"Well, lookie here. Here comes ol' fancy-pants. And it looks like he don't even know how to eat with a fork and a knife. He's got more food on his lap than he got in his gullet."

Thad stopped walking and stared at the window slightly above his head to see the grimy unshaven face staring back at him.

"Hey, he shore do. Too bad the jailer took away our breakfast dishes. We could've had ol' fancy pants scoot up next to these bars here and we could've eaten a good meal right off his shirt."

"Hey, you holding out on us, fancy pants? Usually, I like to wash down my meals with a bottle of red. Where's my bottle?"

Thad turned and walked toward the hotel, ignoring the dirty drunks in the jail cell.

"Oh, my word, what happened to you Mr. Jackson?" Randal Turner said as he left his post behind the registry counter.

"It's a long story, Randal, and I'd rather not go into it at this time. As you can tell, I'll need a hot bath and these clothes I have on will need to be cleaned."

"We'll most certainly take care of you. Why don't you take this." Randal ran to reach under the counter and handed Thaddeus a clean bathrobe, "And place your dirty clothes into this bag." He fished around under the counter and handed Thad a laundry bag.

He was on his way toward the stairs when he heard Randal ring the desk bell.

"Juanita? One of our customers had an accident and needs a hot bath in room 201 right away."

"Yes, Mr. Turner."

"And take Rebeca with you."

"Yes, Mr. Turner."

Thad unlocked the door and closed it behind him. The cool darkness felt soothing against the noise and confusion of the day. He removed his shirt and placed it in the bag then wiped the gravy from his shoes and hoped for the best as he shoved his pants into the bag. He had just wrapped the bathrobe around him when Juanita rapped on the door.

"Bath, sir?"

"Yes, and can you ladies get the clothes inside this bag washed and ironed?"

The girls had no more than left before Thad sank into the warm water and closed his eyes. The cool darkness was a godsend. He didn't care if he found the horses his father wanted. Knowing his father, he'd do that himself whether Thad and Beverly found them or not. The only thing Thad would have to do was sign the paperwork the government would provide. Then, he wouldn't want to know more than that. Once the horses became government property, they would be sent to some overseas, God-forsaken battlefield and die just like their human soldiers.

He didn't know when it happened, but Thad fell asleep and was awakened by Beverly pounding on his door.

Chapter 16

"I hope you can forgive me for what happened this afternoon, Mr. Jackson." The girl was seated inside the wagon with her family.

"Yes, there's nothing to forgive. How are you doing?"

"Oh, I'm fine. I just had a plate of fried chicken and a cup of lemonade dumped in my lap. You were actually punched in the face. That had to hurt."

"I've been punched harder. My father wants to eat a little early." He glanced around and chuckled before grabbing his mouth.

"I'm sorry, laughing still hurts. Would you like to join us? The whole family is welcome."

"Thanks for the invitation," said Matthew, but we have several hours of chores to catch up before we're finished. Caroline is welcome to join you, if she wants." Matthew nodded at her.

"Oh, I'd love to, Thad, but you heard my father. I couldn't live with myself if I knew my family was home doing my chores. Maybe sometime later?"

"Yes..." Thad nodded and smiled. Maybe later." He stood on the plank walkway and watched the wagon disappear down the street.

******

Jack Caldwell was riding in the second row of the posse directly behind Matthew. He had gotten off to a rough start early that morning, with things not going the way he'd planned. He had intended to apologize for his misdeeds at the start of the second posse that very morning, except Thad and his father did not show up for the gathering of the posse. It was Sheriff David Price that got in his face.

"Well, if neither of them were members of the original posse, what made you think they were going to be members of this one. And since you're the one who discovered Bobby's body, you're a member of this posse, like it or not.

"But Mr. Larkin's going to fire me if I can't get "em to forgive me and make things right."

"Again, that's not our problem. You're the one who punched a business man in the kisser just because he was delivering a plate of food to Manhunter's daughter. Getting all swollen up with yourself and punching folks is not the proper way of getting along."

"Neither is claiming to be in love with one woman and making eyes at a different one. None of that will get you very far," Matthew said with a chuckle.

"I wasn't making eyes at anyone."

"Really?" Matthew fished out the makings and began rolling a smoke. "I'll swear in a court of law that you were spying on Beverly Jackson. Now, that's alright, if that's what you meant to do. But just don't expect everyone else to be happy about it." He struck a match on the sole of his boot and lit his cigarette. "You're lucky Caroline didn't cut your heart out."

******

They rode in silence for the majority of the afternoon. The sun had begun to sink low in the western sky when Matthew drew up to a grove of cottonwoods that lined the riverbank and dismounted.

"This is as far as we tracked them."

"And where'd they go?" Benjamin Polk asked as he swung his right leg over the horses' neck and dropped to the ground.

"They crossed the river about a quarter of a mile downstream from here."

"Well then, if they crossed, we can too. Let's mount up and go get 'em."

Several members of the posse voiced their assent as Matthew took a swig from his canteen.

"We could." He hung the canteen on the saddle. "We also could get shot, if they're waiting for us. I don't really know how you guys feel about it, but I'd like to return to my family in one piece."

"But we don't know that they're watching us," Jack said.

"You wanna cross and see if anyone is watching us? Go right ahead and let us know what you find."

"Then what are we going to do?" Jack asked.

"You're going to stop right here, back in the trees, and act like you're settling down for the evening. Then, while everyone is relaxed, I'll ease back the way we came and cross the river back around the bend. There's a shallow place I know where I can cross easily. I'll find out how many there are and how well they're set up. Stay back here and keep away from the river."

"These horses need water," Benjamin said.

"There's a creek about twenty yards or so south of us." Matthew pointed. "Be careful. If we know about the creek, they may also know about it."

"Okay, everyone heard the man," Dave Price said, loud enough to be heard across the river. "Everyone waters their own mount."

Jack untied the reins of his appaloosa as the horse neighed loudly and stamped his hooves.

"Yah, now, cut that out," Jack yelled and tugged on the reins. Instead of quieting down, the appaloosa reared up and pawed the air, causing Jack to scramble.

"Knock it off, you melon-head!"

The other horses were following their riders toward the creek, leaving Jack and the unruly appaloosa to themselves.

Matthew stopped his pinto on a little crest of a hill to watch the struggle. Choosing a good horse was as much a part of learning to be a cowboy as knowing how to rope a young calf or burn a brand. Jack had been quick to claim the appaloosa as his horse early that morning while they were getting outfitted for the posse. It was a big, beautiful animal with a lot of spirit. As far as Matthew was concerned, that was about as far as it went. The animal fought the rider every chance he got and stopped to eat whenever it pleased him. He was also constantly thirsty. In Matthew's opinion, he belonged behind a plow.

The horse's protest grew louder as it reared several more times neighing and snorting. He even charged Jack once, making him scramble away on all fours.

"That's it," Matthew said and tied his pinto to the tree they were standing by. He drew the Sharps rifle from the scabbard and headed toward the melee. As it was, the unruly devil was slowing them down.

He was nearing the bank when a Winchester barked from the opposite side of the river, spinning Jack around and off his feet, landing him in the water. A small cloud of gun smoke clung in the air on the opposite bank and Matthew quickly fired the Sharps at its center. Someone on the opposite bank cursed and fell, breaking several branches and twigs as he retreated.

Matthew grabbed Jack by the shirt collar and dragged him up the bank where the rest of the posse was waiting.

"How bad is he hurt?" Dave asked.

"I don't know," Matthew said as he unbuttoned Jack's shirt. "But I've never seen a good hurt."

"Let me have a look," Albert Meeks said as he knelt beside Matthew. "Clean shot. The bullet passed through the flesh in his right shoulder without hitting a bone or artery that I can see."

"Where'd you learn about medicine, Al?" Dave said.

"When you spend as many years aboard a British frigate as I have, you get to see all kinds of wounds."

"Is he good enough to ride?" Matthew asked.

"Mmm, I don't know that yet. The main thing is to stop the bleeding. Get me some bandages.

Benjamin Polk scrambled up the hill and fished the medical supplies from one of the pack horses as several members of the posse carried Jack to the campsite. Albert rolled up his shirtsleeves and ordered Benjamin to cut several pads to pack the wound with.

"Nah, you're forgetting something Al," Smokey said and pulled a wad of chewing tobacco from his cheek and packed Jack's wounds.

"There you are. It'll stop any infection. We'll pack 'em again tomorrow morning.

******

They made camp near the creek and staked the horses between two cottonwoods. Dave handed out chores and posted guards. It was about ten o'clock when Matthew joined Albert Meeks at Jack's bedroll.

"How's your patient, Doc?" he asked as Albert held the back of his hand to Jack's forehead.

"I'm certainly not a real doctor, and I'm a far cry from being a nurse. But I'd say our patient is running a little bit of a temperature."

"Is that dangerous?"

"I think it could be. It's hard to tell, but I'd get him back to Leon where a real doctor can see him as soon as possible."

"Okay, I was afraid of that."

Matthew crossed the camp to where Dave Price was and the two men conversed quietly for a few minutes before Dave joined them at Jack's bedroll.

"Matt thinks our young patient might be having a difficulty or two. What do you think, Al?"

"Well, as I tried telling our Comanche friend, I'm not a real doctor… not even close."

"We know that, Al. But you're the closest we've got, so what's the prognosis? Is he going to be alright, or should we send him back to Leon?

Albert pursed his lips and stared off into space for a few seconds before speaking.

"I'd say take him back to Leon."

"Okay," Dave said with a firm nod. "But you're going with him. I don't want him dying on the way. I'd never hear the end of it."

The comment brought a chuckle from Matthew's lips.

"Yeah, what was that all about?"

"The night before last a couple of cowboys came riding into town looking for a good time. Well, it was late and the pharmacy and card games were already closed, so they pulled several bottles from their saddlebags and proceeded to get drunker than a pack of skunks. I warned 'em enough. Then two of them started fighting amongst themselves. I tried breaking it up until one of them took a swing at me. So, I whacked him with my pistol. Then the other two jumped on me for hurting their friend. So, I whacked the both of them too."

"And Sue's mad at you for protecting yourself?"

"I guess. She says we're raising a family and she doesn't want her children to become brutes."

Matthew laughed loudly.

"It's a good thing she didn't marry someone like Bill Hickock. He would have shot all three, and then gone back to bed. Does she want you to quit?"

"No… at least she's never said so. She just wants me to be gentle and kinder. I tried explaining that doesn't work when some yahoo's pointing a .45 at you, but she didn't want to listen."

Matthew shook his head and chuckled. "I suppose Vicky might feel the same way, except when it comes to our children. Don't hurt one of our young 'uns, or she'll take after you with our shotgun."

Matthew mounted his horse and surveyed the posse. "Benjamin Polk and Smokey can go with us. The rest go with Albert. I'll show you how to make a travois."

The camp suddenly became a din of activity as the posse members collected and packed their belongings and saddled their horses. Albert Meeks doused the campfire and checked on Jack's condition. Matthew stopped in the middle of saddling his horse and gazed into predawn darkness as Dave joined his side.

"Something wrong, Matt?"

"We're being watched."

"From where?" Dave glanced around quickly.

"From across the river, but also from this side."

"Okay, what's the best way to get 'em?"

"There isn't one. Not unless you want a bunch of dead people on your hands. While we were planning on surprising them in the morning, they were already surprising us."

Dave glanced around once more. "Okay, what do we do in the meantime?"

"We make sure the posse's safely gone before we do anything in the dark. Then, we leave quietly and return later when we know who and what we're dealing with."

Chapter 17

Thaddeus Jackson held the door to Zydeco's Cajun Restaurant open for his daughter and son to enter. New Orleans style food was the last thing he expected to find in Leon, Kansas, but having spent an extended amount of time in New Orleans, the aroma coming from the kitchen told him the food was authentic and it made his mouth water. He had not been introduced to the beautiful middle-aged woman writing the day's special on a chalkboard. She laid the chalk down and came their way.

Yvonne shook her head as she noticed Thad Jr.'s face. "There you are. I was wondering if you were alright. Someone told me some ruffians broke into your hotel room and beat you up." Yvonne gently touched a bruise on Thad Jr.'s cheek and frowned.

"The doctor says I'm healing fine, but thank you for your concern. Yvonne, I'd like to introduce you to our father, Thaddeus Jackson the First. Dad, this is Yvonne… I'm sorry, I don't know your last name."

"It doesn't matter." She gave a throaty chuckle. "You didn't know my last name because I didn't tell you. It is a silly name. But in case you really want to know, it is La Rouge. Come."

Thaddeus Sr. felt a chill sweep through his veins as she motioned them toward an empty table. It had been over a year since he had last seen Yvonne La Rouge, but the spark inside of him was stronger today than it had ever been.

Thad Sr. had a smile tug at the corners of his mouth as they seated themselves. It had been so long since he had seen her, he wondered if she would remember him at all. And since she was doing a fine job of hiding the fact, he decided to play along with her for now.

"You may sit where you wish. You're our only customers today."

"It's early. You'll probably pick up a few more dinners before you're through. And your name is a good French name," he said.

"Thank you, *Monsieur*. That is very kind of you."

The table she sat them at was in a secluded corner of the restaurant that was mostly lit by lamplight. She handed them each a menu. Thaddeus Sr. closed his menu and smiled at her.

"I already know I want the crawfish gumbo with hushpuppies and okra. And my son will need something less spicy, since his mouth is still healing."

"And the young lady?"

"Beverly has a cast-iron stomach. So, whatever she says is fine."

"Dad!" Beverly said and swatted at his arm.

"Well, it's true."

"How about a sample platter with a bit of everything we are serving today?" Yvonne said.

Thad waited until Yvonne had gone to the kitchen before broaching the subject he wanted to discuss.

"So, Dad. What are we going to do about the horses? And please, don't tell me I've got to buy a bunch of animals from Jim Larkin's place. I'm sure Jack Caldwell's still working there."

"Oh, I'm sure he is too, although he's with that posse right now. But we don't have to let him run the show. We simply figure out a way to make him eat crow."

"So, how do we go about doing that?" Beverly asked.

"Well, for one thing, I certainly would not pay any attention to him when he starts barking about that pretty blond-headed girl being his fiancé. She definitely likes you."

"That's what I've been telling him, Dad, but he won't listen," Beverly said, as she scooted closer to the table. Thad grinned. The girl took eating as serious business, but never seemed to gain an ounce.

"You need to listen to you sister, Son."

"No, what I *need* is to get out of Leon, Kansas."

"And why is that? What's throwing up your hands and quitting going to get you?"

Thad heaved a deep sigh and shook his head.

"I don't honestly know what it's going to get me either. I can't even go to a church picnic without getting punched in the face and food dumped all over me."

"Yes," Thaddeus Jackson said with a chuckle. "But then a bunch of very nice people gathered together to help you out. And from what I hear, it happened almost like that the first time, when those guys broke into your room and beat on you. Cotton and Dave tossed them into jail, and Randal Turner stayed late, making sure you two were safe and taken care of."

"When are those guys in the jail going to trial, Pop?" Beverly asked.

"We're just waiting on the judge. My guess is they'll hold the hearing the day after tomorrow."

Thaddeus stopped and cleared his throat as Yvonne came from the kitchen carrying a large platter which she set in the middle of the table.

"This is for the table to share. Then, when you find what you want to eat, the chef will cook it for you." She paused to look at Thad Jr. and smiled. "Except for you. I have something special for you."

She returned to the kitchen as Beverly shoveled a forkful of rice into her mouth.

"Okay, back to what we were discussing," Thad said, but was waved off by his father as Yvonne returned from the kitchen carrying a plate of chopped fruit smothered with a sweet creamy sauce and sat it in front of Thad.

"For you. It is cool and soothing. It will help with the healing."

She gently squeezed his shoulder and left to seat several more customers that had just come in.

"Okay, now we can get back to what we were discussing," Thad said.

"Not so fast, my boy. Never spoil a good meal with business."

"I thought you used to take clients out to lunch or supper," Beverly said before sampling the chicken gumbo.

"I still do," Thaddeus said with a nod. "But I always keep the subject we discuss during those meals circled in on their children or maybe sports, like fishing. I make it a habit to bounce business around as we are getting ready to leave, and that for just a few minutes. I always make more friends and money that way."

******

Thaddeus Jackson paid his bill and left a generous gratuity for Yvonne while Thad and Beverly waited outside. Someone started ringing the fire bell and Beverly elbowed her way to the edge of the sidewalk as a crowd began to gather. Several members of the posse had entered the city from the north and were headed their way. One of the horses was pulling a travois carrying a man with a bloody bandage on his chest. The crowd pushed her forward as the horses stopped in front of Doc Williams' office. Beverly felt her heart break and she heaved a sob as she recognized Jack Caldwell on the travois.

Chapter 18

Albert Meeks slid off his horse and rushed into the doctor's office, returning with the doctor a few seconds later. Dr. Williams glanced at Jack Caldwell before ordering two of the men to carry Jack inside his surgery room. He started to follow but stopped when he saw Beverly standing by the travois and motioned for her to follow.

"Mrs. Williams is still visiting her sister in Detroit and I can use your help."

She looked back over her shoulder and her father waved her on. She entered the doctor's office as Albert Meeks was explaining to the doctor and Sheriff Blankenship how Jack had gotten shot.

"That's good. We can work with that. Why don't you step outside and tell that bunch blocking the sidewalk the same thing. It'll save Dave and me a lot of work," Sheriff Blankenship said.

******

"Put your handbag and umbrella over in that corner and grab a surgical robe from the closet," Dr. Williams said as he poured what Beverly would have sworn was whiskey into a tray with his surgical instruments.

The robe swallowed her and she solved part of the problem by cuffing and rolling the sleeves up past her elbows and taping them in position. Jack moaned, causing her to hover close to his head.

"He isn't in any danger right now, so you can relax," Dr. Williams said with a chuckle. "Right now, let's get him cleaned up and get started. See if you can remove his boots while I work on his shirt. I want you to be my anesthesiologist today."

Beverly paused in her tracks and stared at the doctor.

"What is a...an anesthesiologist? I've never heard of such a thing."

"Don't worry, I'll teach you." He cut the shirt in two and threw it in the trash can. "You will be the one giving him medicine to relieve pain. We could do it the old-fashioned way of having our patient take a drink of whiskey and bite down on a stick, but I'm afraid you wouldn't find that appealing."

He unlocked a cabinet and removed a bottle that he held high.

"A few drops of this and our friend here will be sleeping like a baby."

Beverly fell into the role of being whatever Doctor Williams needed at that moment and gladly accepted the doctor's praise when they finished. She rehung the surgical robe back in the closet as Dr. Williams opened all the windows.

"A few more minutes of breathing ether fumes and I'm afraid we all would be taking naps." He gave her a grin and adjusted his glasses. "What you need to do is go to a restaurant and drink a big glass of orange juice and eat a little snack to get your sugar level back up."

"What about you, doctor?" Beverly protested. "You were doing all the work."

"I will be doing the same thing as soon as my daughter gets here. "Run along now."

Beverly stood in the door to the doctor's office buttoning her coat as a scrap of paper bounced off her right shoe and rattled down the street with a gust of wind. The black clouds boiling over the hills told her a storm was on its way. She started to cross the street toward Zydeco's when Caroline Blue walked her pinto to the hitching rail in front of the doctor's office and dismounted.

"I expected you earlier," Beverly said and grabbed her in a hug.

"I just found out an hour ago, then my horse threw a shoe. How is he?"

"Jack is going to be fine. Would you like to see him?"

"Sure, if they will let us in."

"They'd better. I was the one who assisted Dr. Williams through surgery," Beverly said as Caroline opened the door.

"You were his nurse?"

"Yes, I was. He called me his anesthesiologist."

Dr. Williams poked his head out of the back room and said, "I'm sorry girls, but Jack needs rest. Can you come back to see him later tonight? Or better yet, tomorrow."

"But can't she at least look at him for just a minute? They're supposed to get married."

"Ah, so you're the unlucky young lady, huh Caroline? Okay, but let him sleep, and just for a minute."

Caroline walked silently to Jack's side and gazed at him. His skin color was pale and she felt her heart skip a beat as he winced, then she relaxed as he seemed to settle down.

"Okay, ladies, time to go. You both may return later, say around six or seven. But it will still be on a limited basis."

"Thank you, Doctor. Thank you so much for what you've done." Both girls hugged him before slipping quietly out the door. Beverly grabbed Caroline's hand and started dragging her toward Zydeco's.

"Wait, Beverly. I've got to get Laughing Brook to Smokey so he can look at her, or I'll be sleeping in the street tonight."

"You'll do no such thing. We'll take your horse to the blacksmith, but if it gets late, you'll share my hotel room."

Caroline laughed and draped an arm around Beverly's shoulder as they walked toward the Blacksmith.

"I'm afraid I might be a little dirtier than you think. I was mucking out stalls when they told me about the shooting."

"It doesn't matter," Beverly said matter-of-factly. "The hotel has a brass tub in my room."

"They'll let you bathe inside the rooms?"

"Of course they will, silly," Beverly said. "At least they'd better for what my dad's paying them. Yesterday afternoon I got a little hungry, so I told Randal Turner at the desk and fifteen minutes later I had a fish sandwich with pickles and dressing."

"No kidding! Was it good?"
"Of course it was."

.

******

Laughing Brook had not only thrown her left rear shoe, but had gotten a stone bruise.

"I'm sorry, Caroline," Jason Walker said as he gently bathed Laughing Brook's hoof. Jason was taking care of the horses at the livery while Smokey was out with the posse. "She's a fine horse and she should heal quickly. But I'd refrain from riding her for a while until the swelling goes down. I can lend you one of the stable horses to get you back home, but it's getting late and you might want to wait until the morning."

"That's okay, Jason. I'll take her home tomorrow." Caroline reached into a basket and gave Laughing Brook an apple.

"My parents definitely need to have a telephone installed," she mumbled.

"That's right," Beverly said as she took Caroline's arm. "I didn't see one the night we stayed at your house. "If your dad's going into business with my pop, he'll need to have one installed."

"Does your dad use one a lot?"

"You ought to see him. It's like watching a baby sucking on a sugar tit."

They entered the hotel where Beverly marched straight toward the main desk.

Chapter 19

Matthew rose in the pre-dawn blackness and quietly shook out a pair of moccasins he had pulled from his bedroll then slipped them on. He picked up the Sharps and, carrying it in his right hand, he strolled quickly toward a large clump of brush and trees then disappeared into the night. He picked up the pace and settled into a ground-eating jog that had him reaching the shallow bend in the river in a matter of minutes. He unstrapped his gun belt and draped it over his shoulders, then stepped quietly into the water. He had always figured it was easier to slip up on someone this time of day, especially when they'd been on guard-duty all night. They would be groggy and fighting sleepy eyes.

The cold river made a noise like silk around his ankles as he slipped from the bank to mid-stream, then to the opposite bank and up into the brush. He shrunk back as several birds took off and upward with a squawk. After a couple of minutes of silence, Matthew crept forward, moving from tree to bush to boulder. He came to a complete halt when he almost bumped into a man who was sleeping with his jacket drawn around himself against the cold. Matthew quickly grabbed a hunk of wood at his feet and slammed it against the side of the man's head. He fell like a sack of grain while Matthew shrunk back into the brush.

Matthew pulled a leather thong from his belt and tied the unconscious man to the tree he had been leaning against then stuffed his bandana into his mouth.

"There, you be a good boy and take a nap," he whispered and moved away.

It was beginning to get lighter now, and he'd have to move faster. He crept up higher and peered back at the meager campsite below. It looked as though two more rustlers were asleep by a cold campfire. The spot they chose to corral the stolen cattle had plenty of water and grass. It would have been the perfect spot, if the cattle were not stolen. Which brought another question to Matthew's mind. What were they waiting for? All the rustlers he had dealt with before were in a hurry to unload their stolen livestock, but this band looked like they were in for the long haul.

He had originally braced himself for an old-fashioned gunfight between the rustlers and the posse, but what he had inherited was much easier. He chose a comfortable spot between a small tree and a boulder and checked the load in the rifle. Someone was busy building a campfire in the posse camp across the river. From where he lay, it didn't look more than two hundred yards between the stolen cattle and the posse.

There were two men up and rolling their bedrolls in the posse camp now.

Matthew took careful aim and pulled the double triggers on the Sharps. The gun roared and the rustler's coffee pot was sent spinning through the air. The rustlers scrambled around on all fours, trying to figure where the bullet came from. One of the men finally noticed the cloud of gun smoke and fired his pistol. Matthew fired again, hitting the man in the thigh. He fell with a howl and rolled on the ground cursing.

The other rustler decided to make a run for the river but ran headlong into Dave Price and the posse. He turned back but Matthew fired the Sharps once more, kicking up dirt and gravel several inches from the man's toes.

"Drop your guns and raise your hands, boys," Matthew yelled. "Your guard up here in the rocks is kinda tied up right now and can't help you. I could kill every one of you from right here."

The man carefully laid his pistol on the bedroll and knelt with his hands in the air. Matthew waited for Dave and his posse to surround the men, then went to untie the look-out. He pulled the scarf from the man's mouth and was rewarded with several profane names, so Matthew stuffed it back in his mouth.

"You'd best keep that right there for your own health. Now, move!" Matthew gave him a shove.

"Well, well. Here's our one-man posse," Dave said with a growl. "Why didn't you tell the rest of us your plan?"

"Because I didn't really have one until I got up on the hill above them. Then…" Matthew shrugged his shoulders. "It was so easy, I'm almost afraid to take any credit."

"Hey, Dave. What are we going to do with this guy that Matt shot? He's bleeding like a stuck pig," Benjamin Polk said.

"I don't know. Wrap it up and lets go."

Chapter 20

"Hi Randy. Are there any messages for my father?" Beverly leaned across the counter and batted her eyes.

"Yes, ma'am." He quickly thumbed through a stack of papers and handed a note-sized slip of paper to her. "Judge Wilson says he wants to conduct a hearing concerning those men who beat your brother up at ten o'clock tomorrow morning. And this package came for Miss Caroline." He reached under the desk and handed her a package wrapped in paper and tied with twine.

"Oh," Caroline said as she pulled a corner of the paper back. "It looks like my dress. I wonder if they got all the stain out?"

"Well, unwrap it and let's find out," Beverly said with a literal bounce in her step.

Randal quickly cleared the counter then Caroline used his scissors to cut the twine.

"Oh, wow! It looks pretty good," Beverly said.

"Let me see it," Randal said and lifted the collar to inspect it more closely. "I'd say it's almost perfect. I found one little spot here," he lifted the collar and pointed. "There's a little staining right here."

"Yeah, but no one's ever going to see it, Randy."

She turned and held it against Caroline's body. "Well, there's your dress tonight."

"Not unless I can get rid of the mucking smell."

"Can you be a good boy, Randy, and send up some bathwater?"

"Of course I can," he said with a laugh.

******

Caroline sank slowly into the hot bath water and submerged her head before applying soap to her skin. She remembered growing up that she was never able to bathe in clean bathwater that had not carried her younger brother's dirt before she climbed into the tub. Well, there was a time before Mark was crawling around getting into things that she bathed in clean water, but that wasn't too long and seventeen years of dirty water was more than enough. But of course, her mother and Matthew both bathed last, so she shouldn't feel too sorry for herself.

"Here, I want you to try this." Beverly held a bottle with a screw-on cap in front of Caroline's nose.

"It's shampoo for your hair. I use it all the time. It keeps my hair soft and shiny. Let me show you."

Beverly poured a small amount into her palm and started working it into Caroline's scalp. Before long the small amount of shampoo turned into a fluffy mound on Caroline's head.

"It smells like strawberries," Caroline said.

"Yes, and I have another bottle that smells like oranges." She poured clean water over Caroline's head as she talked. "My father has a lot of women who try to get him interested or win his heart for themselves. Sometimes they bring gifts for me."

"Are any of them pretty?" Caroline asked as she stood and grabbed a towel.

"Oh yes. I mean there are a few who I wouldn't want my dog to marry, but yes," Beverly grabbed an extra towel and began drying Caroline's hair. "There are some really pretty ones chasing after Dad. One in particular always smells like a bouquet of flowers. I liked being around her. She told me it was always important for a woman to smell good."

"That sounds about right," Caroline said with a laugh. "A man can go around town flirting with women, smelling like chewing tobacco and whiskey, but they want their women to smell like flowers."

"You can always do what I do," Beverly said with a chuckle.

"What's that?"

"I tell them right to their face they stink. If they're interested in me, they'll take a bath and clean their teeth. If they won't do that…" she shrugged, "good luck on finding anyone who'll put up with them."

"My dad had to arrest a woman once who smelled like an old outhouse, so I guess it goes two ways."

Someone tried opening the door before pounding on it. "Hey, Beverly, open the door."

Beverly gave Caroline a crooked grin. "My brother can be a pest." She turned toward the door and yelled. "Yeah, what do you want?"

"Dad says he wants to have supper earlier tonight. Are you decent?" He wiggled the door handle once more."

"No! I have Caroline Blue with me and she's taking a bath. Tell Dad we'll be there as soon as we can."

"Okay, but don't be too late. You know how he gets."

"You go ahead, Beverly. I'll be okay," Caroline said as she ran a brush through her hair.

"No, I'm staying with you." Beverly opened the window overlooking the patio. "Sit here." She patted the leather-bound chair. "Now, lean out the window."

Caroline instantly felt the wind tugging at her hair.

"Here, let me have that." Beverly took the brush from Caroline's hand and began brushing the long blond hair. "I discovered this the other day when my dad was waiting for me. Relax. Randy says the wind's always blowing on this end of the building. No one knows why, but it really makes it easy to dry your hair."

******

Vicky Blue stood beside her son, reading the note in the middle of the table. 'What do you think it means, Ma?" Mark said.

"Probably means exactly what it says. Someone shot Jack Caldwell and they were taking him to Doc Williams' office."

Mark grabbed Rose around the waist as she darted toward the open door. She gave him a good giggle as he tossed her in the air and caught her.

"Are we going to head back into town to see what condition he's in?"

Vicky walked to the door and stared at the farm outside. "No, Mark. We have too many chores to do, and we're two hands short now. We'll get up early and go to town then. In the meantime, what do you want for supper?"

Chapter 21

"Here ye, hear ye! The City of Leon Municipal Court is now in session, the honorable Judge Silas Wilson presiding. All rise." Acting bailiff Sheriff David Price rapped the gavel loudly.

Silas seated himself behind the podium and nodded toward the crowd. "You may be seated." The tiny courtroom might have held fifty or sixty people on a normal court day, but today the room was packed to almost double its capacity. Caroline was certain the only reason she was seated in the prime seat she was in was because she had entered the courtroom with Beverly, who was a witness, at her side. Beverly took the last empty seats next to Thaddeus Jackson and a couple of high-priced solicitors. The four defendants were chained together and were seated between the judge and the spectators. Judge Wilson sniffed several times as he looked around the room.

"Sheriff Blankenship?"

"Yes, Your Honor?" The sheriff leaned the shotgun he'd been holding against the wall before facing the judge.

"What is that putrid smell? Do we have some dead animal underneath this building?"

"No sir. What we have is four of the dirtiest men I've ever seen, and that's saying a lot. They refused to bathe the whole time they were locked up in jail, and refused to bathe before showing up in court today."

"Is that right? Well, what do you men have to say for yourselves?"

"Well, we just figured if you heard our story, you'd turn us loose and collect our fines from them rich folks," one of the men said and the other three laughed.

Silas rapped the gavel several times and pointed toward the men. "You just might want to listen to me, since I'm the one who will decide your fate. This ain't no three-ringed jury trial you're in. It's my court and I decide what goes on here. You're being charged with breaking and entering at the hotel, and also breaking into Thaddeus Jackson's room, where you beat him half to death. What do you have to say for yourselves?"

"Well, we didn't mean no harm, Judge. We'd been drinking all day and…"

"Kansas is a dry state. Where'd you get the moonshine?"

"We brung it with us. We figured on selling some of it."

"Bootlegging? Do any of you have a solicitor?"

"I hope not! I don't even know what that word means," the one who had given Thaddeus the beating said, then he laughed.

Judge Wilson's demeanor changed as he began writing.

"Well, since I can't stand being in the same room with you four smelling the way you do, I will tell you what I am going to do. I will appoint you an attorney to represent the four of you. I am also authorizing Sheriff

Blankenship to see that you are bathed, shaven and have on freshly washed clothes. Court is adjourned until ten o'clock tomorrow morning."

He slammed his gavel against the podium and rose to his feet. One of the men started to complain, but the judge turned his back on him and started a conversation with one of Thaddeus' attorneys.

"Danged idiots! I've never seen anything like it. They smell worse than the hogs I raise and the hogs are smarter."

Sheriff Blankenship rattled the keys to the jail cells and motioned for Smokey to join him. "Here," he said handing the shotgun to Smokey. It's loaded, so make sure where it's pointed. But I want you to unload both barrels if they even pretend to escape."

"Okay, boss. I used to carry one of these every day back when I worked for Wells Fargo."

Sheriff Blankenship handed the key ring to the big man who was acting like a spokesman.

"Here, unlock your ankles and let's go."

The man threw the keys across the room, hitting Judge Wilson between the shoulder blades. Sheriff Blankenship took a step forward and brought the heel of his boot down on the man's foot. He bellowed like a wounded bull and crumbled to the floor.

"I'm sorry about that, Your Honor. I guess our smelly friend here wants to go back to jail."

"Well then, oblige him.

The man cursed loudly. "You broke my foot!"

"And I'm going to break your face if you don't shut up."

"Bootlegging, breaking and entering, assaulting a guest at the hotel, assaulting a judge in the line of duty, and profanity in a public building. The list is getting longer," Judge Wilson said. "You and your friends will be building roads for the State of Kansas for a long time."

"You're crazy. I never attacked any judge, counting you."

"Oh, but you did," Sheriff Blankenship said. "I saw you throw the heavy keyring that hit the honorable Judge Silas Wilson in the back, causing him much pain and distress."

"That's all a lie!" he yelled.

"Prove it. Who do you think the townspeople will believe tomorrow in court?" Harvey Blankenship laughed as he grabbed the man's collar and walked him toward the door. "Now, you're going to take a bath even if I have to get some men to strip you naked in the middle of Main Street and turn the fire hose on you. You get to decide which it's going to be. The laundry or naked on Main Street?"

They stopped at the laundry and the prisoner poked his head through the door and pulled back.

"There ain't nothing but washtubs women wash clothes in."

"Yeah, kind of fitting wouldn't you say? Now, get undressed and climb in."

"We'll also need their names and where they're from before we're finished,"

Sheriff Blankenship glanced over his shoulder before stepping aside to reveal Judge Silas leading a growing crowd as they followed behind.

"You heard that, didn't you? Say yes." Harvey used his grip on the collar for force a nod. "You can tell me your real name any time you want."

"Go to hell!"

"No sir, I've already saddled my bronc next to Jesus and that's where I'm staying. Now, you want to try that again? What's your full name?" Cotton gave him a shove, causing him to stumble over the threshold.

The man screamed several curses at cotton.

"My, my, my." Cotton slapped him hard on the cheek. "Hush that kind of talk. There are women and children present. Now, are you going to get undressed, or do you want me to cut them rags off your back."

"You can't do that."

"No? You heard what the judge ordered me to do." Cotton pulled his hunting knife and "Now, what's it going to be?"

Beads of sweat formed on the man's face as he watched Cotton check the edge of the blade with his thumb.

"Still no? Okay…" Cotton motioned for Albert Meeks to join him as he stepped inside. Albert grabbed a wooden plunger from one of the tubs and the man hollered.

"My name's Cherry Michaels and I'm from Arizona!"

"Now, see how easy that was. We're getting somewhere now," Cotton said, as he leaned against the door post.

******

Once Cotton discovered the big man's name was Cherry Michaels from Arizona, the dam seemed to burst. He had the names of all four defendants and their places of birth. Cotton quickly sent telegrams and just as quickly received warrants on three of the men.

He looked up from his desk as Beverly poked her head inside. "Come see this!" She pointed outside.

When he looked, he saw Manhunter and Dave Price arriving back in town with three prisoners with their hands tied behind their backs. One of them was leaning in the saddle and had a bloody bandage wrapped around his leg.

When Cotton approached them, Matthew said, "We've got to get this man to the doc and we'll be back to fill you in.

Chapter 22

"I don't think any one of them is very intelligent," Beverly said as she took a sip of red wine.

They were sitting at a row of tables inside Zydeco's, next to Matthew and Vicky and their children. Cotton and Alice were also invited. It was Thaddeus Jackson's way of saying *thanks* for closing a business deal concerning the sale of forty-nine horses from Matthew's ranch, and another sixty horses from the Larkin Ranch. They were waiting for their food to arrive when the conversation had turned to the sanity of the defendants.

"Albert Meeks and me pulled a decaying rat from the lining in Cherry's jacket," Cotton said. "No telling what else is in there."

"Please, no more at the dinner table," Alice said, and received a vote of agreement from the women.

"I happen to agree with you, daughter," Thaddeus said as he poured a glass of wine for Alice Blankenship. "But when did you start drinking wine?"

"The night when Thad got beat up. Do you really want to discuss that now, Dad?"

"Yes, I do. Since my fourteen-year-old daughter decided to drink a glass of wine in front of me, I think it's a perfect time to discuss the drinking issue."

"My dad and sister have this discussion every time she mentions drinking, or women smoking, or especially the latest in women's fashions," Thad said with a crooked grin.

"Well, some of the fashions coming to us from France are ungodly monstrosities," Thaddeus said. "I saw a lady in Chicago last week who was wearing a dress that revealed her kneecaps. Can you believe that?"

"Well, Dad, that's the way things are going to be, so you'll have to get used to it," Beverly said with a snicker.

"I happen to agree with your pa on this one," Cotton said as he sipped his coffee. "But I've seen enough to know you're probably right."

"What do you think, Mrs. Blankenship?" Beverly said. "You are politically involved."

"Yes, I am. But I'm also torn between having to dress in layers of petticoats that cover the ankles on a hot summer day, and being able to vote or give my opinion inside a room full of men."

"I think you just did." Cotton leaned to kiss her on the cheek.

"Yes, but you're married to me. You have to listen. Ask Vicky, she'll tell you."

"Well, how about it, Mrs. Blue? Do you agree with Mrs. Blankenship?" Thaddeus grinned as he poured more wine.

Vicky took her time sipping water before she answered.

"Well yes, I do… on most things. Take a look at our daughters. Both of them are beautiful young women, and those dresses look marvelous on them. But underneath those dresses are several layers of petticoats, not counting the rest of the unmentionables. The day of Ida Ollar's funeral, the thermometer in Walker's store read over one hundred degrees. I honestly thought I was going to die. In that case I agree with Caroline. All eyes at the table gravitated toward Caroline.

She put her water glass down and cleared her throat. "I will admit to leaving several layers of petticoats out of an ensemble from time to time, but when I'm dressed like a Comanche, I am a Comanche."

"I must have missed something," Vivian Larkin said. "Could you please repeat what you said?"

"What she's saying, Vivian, is most Comanche women go all natural under their skirts," Alice said with a chuckle.

"It's actually not a bad way of life, Vivian," Alice said as she dumped a spoonful of sugar into her coffee cup. "There are fewer clothes to wash and you're cooler. I know I've considered it myself a time or two."

"But… my word," Vivian stammered. "Who's ever thought of such a thing?"

"The Comanche women think the same thing about white women." Caroline took a sip of wine as Yvonne brought a tray loaded with food from the kitchen.

"Okay, you're going to love this." Thaddeus took a large spoonful of brazed pork and passed the bowl to Cotton. "I had the pleasure of spending several weeks in New Orleans awhile back, and this is as close as it gets to genuine Cajun food."

The room became noticeably quieter as Yvonne made several trips to the kitchen for more dishes or wine. They were about halfway through the meal when Cotton shifted to stare at Thaddeus.

"You never got an answer to your question, did you?"

Thaddeus wiped his lips on a napkin and glared at Beverly at the opposite end of the table. "No, I didn't. Would you care to try that again?"

"No, I wouldn't, because you're my dad and there's no way I can win."

"Okay," Thaddeus sat back in his chair and sipped his wine. "I'm feeling generous tonight. Tell me your side of the argument, and if you can win the hearts of the people around the table, I will abide by their decision. But, if they rule against you, then you'll abide by their decision. Is it a deal?"

"Certainly, Beverly said over the top of her glass. "I think it's unfair that Thad can drink wine and I can't, when there's only five years difference in our ages. Caroline told me that most Comanche girls are married by the time they're fourteen, or maybe sixteen years old. I could get married and bear children, but I can't drink a glass of wine? Really? I guess I could grab a gun and kill an intruder, kind of like what I did with my fingernails, but I still can't drink a glass of wine."

She sat back and grinned. "That's all I have to say."

"The only argument I have against your drinking wine is the danged stuff is supposed to be illegal in this state," Cotton said.

"Yeah, how about that, Sheriff?" Alice Blankenship said with a laugh.

"Well, can you imagine eating a meal like this without a glass of wine?" Cotton said. "I think Mark is the only one who doesn't have one."

"That's because my ma said I can't have one."

"Okay," Thaddeus said clearing his throat. "All of you who agree with Beverly, raise your hands." Eleven hands shot up and Beverly released a squeal of victory.

"It seems you won this election, my dear. Just remember, it's all contingent on your behavior. If you drink too much and act like a fool, you'll lose the privilege."

"That's okay, Pops. You'll never have to worry about that."

******

The party lasted much later than Thaddeus thought it might. He told his children goodnight and kissed Beverly on the cheek, then crossed the street to Zydeco's and rapped on the door.

"Mr. Jackson!" Yvonne said as she poked her head through the partially opened door. "Did you forget something?"

"Yes, I did." Thaddeus said, as he squeezed inside and hung his jacket on the coat hanger then began rolling up his sleeves.

"What are you doing?"

"I only rented your restaurant for three hours and look— It's eleven o'clock. The least I could do is help clean the place up."

"No, you've done enough already."

Thaddeus kept sweeping as Yvonne grabbed at the broom. "Where's your father?"

"My father wasn't feeling well, so I sent him to bed. It will only take me a few minutes to finish if you will let me have my broom."

Thaddeus released the broom and touched her shoulder. "What is your father's illness?"

A deep sadness swept over Yvonne and she took her time answering.

"A doctor in New Orleans said he has a problem with his heart. But at first, he was so big and strong, it was hard to tell."

"Mary Jane was the same way," Thaddeus said with a nod. "The hardest lesson for me to learn was that I couldn't stop the cancer from attacking her body. No matter how hard I worked or how much money I donated to research, I couldn't stop her cancer."

Yvonne sighed deeply. "I thought the doctor was wrong at first. Now, I think he's dying… little by little."

He wanted to hold her, but instead he said, "This cleanup will be even faster if you will let me help you,"

Yvonne quit fighting him as they cleaned the tables, swept and mopped the floor. He rinsed the mop and pail and locked them inside a small janitorial closet as Yvonne pulled the cashbox from under the counter.

"I thank you once again. You really were a big help."

"It was my pleasure." Thaddeus placed both hands on her shoulders as he turned to face her. Without hesitating, he leaned over and brushed her lips with his. She seemed to relax as he did it a second time. Thaddeus slipped his left hand behind her neck and his right hand around her waist. She allowed her body to melt against his as an "mmm" escaped her throat and the kiss lasted much longer.

"What are you wanting, Monsieur?"

"I beg your pardon?"

"Most men, when they discover I'm a forty-two-year-old widow, want me in their bed. I've had them offer me money, but I never took their money, and I won't allow this to continue if that's all you want." She took in a deep breath and exhaled. I'll ask you again. What are you after?"

"Would it surprise you to learn that growing up I had one girlfriend and I married her. We stayed married and raised two children until the day she died. I know I'm not the world's greatest catch, but I'm tired of being alone at night. What little time we had in New Orleans last year, and what we've had the past few days here in Leon… what I really want is you. Will you marry me, Yvonne La Rouge?"

Yvonne gave a throaty laugh as she wrapped her arms around Thaddeus' waist and held him tightly.

"When?"

"I beg your pardon?"

"When do you wish to marry me?"

"Tonight, if we can wake the judge this time of night."

Yvonne laughed again as she looked him in the face. "I don't think waking Judge Wilson would be such a good idea. Why don't we wait until tomorrow, and we could have Pastor Billings marry us."

Chapter 23

Caroline leaned against a hitching post in front of the hotel, enjoying the cool breeze. Her family had left for home long ago and Caroline was going to become the school's substitute teacher in the morning. Beverly was being entertained by the group of cowboys she and Thad had met in El Dorado. The familiar sound of a fiddle and a guitar floated toward them, only tonight someone had joined them with a harmonica. They were currently playing *The Arkansas Traveler*.

"Mind if I join you?"

Caroline jerked as she turned to see Thad standing next to her.

"Oh… sorry; you caught me by surprise. No, there's plenty of railing left. Help yourself." She inhaled deeply and released it slowly. "I was just enjoying the cool air."

"Yes." Thad mimicked her deep-breathing with a short breath. "Sometimes during the hottest part of the day, I think I'm going to burn up.

"I've often wondered how you stood that dress jacket. If you're too hot, why don't you take it off?"

"When our father told Beverly and I to pack for the trip, he didn't tell us *what* to pack. Neither of us had ever been beyond the streets of Chicago." He shook his head and laughed. "Well, I take that back; I did leave home when I went to college, but that was to a live-in campus with a dress code."

"Huh," Caroline cocked her head in wonderment. "I thought I was the one with overly protective parents."

"No, I think I've got you beat."

They stared at the almost deserted street as the breeze blew a scrap of newspaper past them and Thad reached down to snag it. He brushed a wrinkle out and held it up to read.

"Hmm, yesterday's news. You want it?"

"No," Caroline said with a laugh. "Why would I want it?"

"Lots of reasons," he said as he wadded the paper and shoved it into a waste basket near the hotel door. "You might not have read the paper yesterday because you didn't have a copy, and now you do."

"I will admit, I never thought of that before. I'll have to remember that one."

Their conversation carried them from one thing we should remember to another, until Caroline caught herself stifling a yawn.

"Oh, gosh, I wonder where that came from?"

"It is after eleven o'clock," Thad said as he craned his neck to see the grandfather clock in the hotel lobby.

"Really? I really need to get to bed. I've got to teach school tomorrow."

A peal of girlish laughter came from the clump of people near the other end of the hotel.

"It doesn't look as though she's ready to call it quits, does it?" Caroline said. "But I have to go to bed and she's got the room key."

"Well, so do I." Thad reached into his pocket and dangled a shiny key in front of her.

"Come on, I'll escort you to your room then try to fetch my sister."

He climbed the stairs beside her then unlocked his hotel room door.

"Beverly and I have adjoining rooms. The door you want is in the middle of the wall, there," he pointed. Now, I'll wait here until you make sure she left the door unlocked."

"Thank you."

Caroline skipped past the bed and opened the door. She gave a little wave and closed it. Thad turned to go fetch his sister from the band of cowboys when Beverly's door swung open.

"Thank you, Thad. I enjoyed this evening."

She bounced up on her toes and gave him a little peck on the cheek. Thad grabbed her shoulders and kissed her cheek. They stood in the hallway staring at each other until Caroline leaned in and kissed him on the lips.

"Goodnight, Thad. I really enjoyed this evening.

Chapter 24

"Not anytime soon," Doctor Williams said. He had just been asked by Sheriff Price when the man with the wounded leg could be moved.

"And why not?"

"Because I might have to amputate his leg. That cannon Matthew Blue uses does quite a bit of damage."

"What kind of damage are we talking about, Doc?" Cotton asked as he packed his pipe with fresh tobacco.

"I won't really know until I go fishing around. The worse would be a shattered bone, but I won't be able to tell until I open him up and see what we find. Matthew's gun makes a fairly large hole to patch."

"Hum," Matthew said as he licked the cigarette he had just rolled. "As I saw it from where I sat behind the rock, he was shooting at me, so I shot back, and I'm a better shot. End of story. Of course, I guess I could've asked him where he wanted to get shot."

"No one's blaming you, Matt," Cotton said. "I would've done the same thing."

"I wonder what the Comanche would do if they had a similar situation." Smokey said as he sliced a sliver off a brick of chewing tobacco and plopped it into his cheek.

"I don't follow you, Smokey," Dave said.

"Well, you know. Let's say a band of them got in a tussle with some white men, and one of the white men got wounded. Would they slow things down 'til the wounded guy got well enough to stand trial?" Smokey finished with a nod.

"No, I'm afraid my relatives are a little more direct than white people. They'd more than likely scalp the wounded man and see that the rest received a similar fate."

"Well, we'd best collect our smelly friends and get over to the courthouse. The judge will want to start court in about a half an hour."

"Will you need someone to man the shotgun today, Sheriff?"

"I'll always need a hand with a shotgun, Smokey." Dr. Williams shook his head as the group of men made their way toward the jailhouse.

"Say, wouldn't it be a mess if someday one of us had to use the shotgun inside the courtroom?" Smokey said. "It'd shore be one messy situation."

"Up close? It'd make that Sharps of Matt's look like a popgun." Cotton's voice faded in with the crowd.

******

Thaddeus poked his head into his son's room as he tied his necktie. "I'm afraid you're going to be a little late, if you wanted breakfast."

"Why, what time is it?" Beverly said as she used the conjoining door to enter Thad's room.

"It's nine-thirty right now," Thaddeus said looking at his gold pocket watch. "You might grab a couple of rolls and a mug of coffee from the hotel lobby."

"That's a great idea, Dad. I forgot to set my alarm last night," Thad said as he slipped on a dress shoe. "George Bennett assured me this trial should only last a couple of hours, then we'll be free."

"Yes, he told me the same thing a few minutes ago. But, when you're dealing with laws and courts, there is always the chance of something going wrong. Better hurry now."

Thaddeus turned away, then bounced right back.

"Oh, by the way, I might be a little late, but I'll be there. So, save me two seats."

"Wait, Dad? Where are you going?" Beverly said as she followed him down the hall.

"You'll find out as soon as possible. Now, run along and make sure that the both of you are on time. You're key witnesses in this hearing."

******

Judge Silas Wilson woke in a cranky mood and he didn't want to be trifled with, regardless. Actually, it was a lack of sleep causing the misery. One of Silas' prized sows became deathly ill and Silas had stayed up nursing her. When he looked across the podium at Cherry Michaels and his three friends, the look of distain on his face was too strong to hide.

"Sheriff Blankenship?"

"Yes, Your Honor?"

"I thought I wrote out a court order appointing George Pollock to represent those four men in today's proceedings."

"You did, Your Honor."

"Then, where is he?"

"He's in Missouri visiting his brother who got hurt in a farming accident."

"And I suppose it wasn't important enough for someone to come and tell me?"

"I would have, Your Honor, except I didn't find out where he was until early this morning."

The judge fumbled with a packet of papers on the podium before rising to his feet.

"You may be seated. I'll be in my chambers and will let you know of my decision."

Thad and Beverly shifted their chairs so they could see one another and opened the small paper bag containing breakfast rolls. Thad stopped with a roll halfway to his mouth and stared.

"What's wrong, brother?" Beverly shifted to see what Thad was gawking at and almost dropped her roll. Their father had just entered the courtroom escorting Yvonne on his arm. Thad jumped to his feet as they approached their seats.

"Dad… Miss La Rouge… What are you doing?"

"What do you mean, what we are doing?" Thaddeus said with a laugh. "It dawned on me late last night that no one had given Yvonne a tour of a working courtroom, so I decided to correct the situation."

"She can have my chair if she wants," Thad said and bumped into several people as he clamored to his feet.

"That is very kind of you, Monsieur Thad," Yvonne said as she sat in his chair.

"If I had known, I would have brought you a roll from the hotel," Beverly said.

"Oh, that's okay. I ate breakfast with my father."

"Since your father is a chef, what does he enjoy eating?" Beverly said.

"Yes, my papa does create food everyone enjoys eating. But he likes simple food, like I cook. This morning we had fried eggs, ham and fried potatoes with onions. But my father isn't feeling well today, so we won't be opening Zydeco's today."

"Has he seen a doctor?" Thad asked.

"No, Monsieur. I'm afraid doctors charge money for their services, and money is something we don't have. But it comes and goes, so tomorrow he will probably feel good and we will open Zydeco's again."

Thad stared at the roll in his hand before tossing it back into the paper sack. The door to the Judge's chamber opened and everyone inside the courtroom rose to their feet with a roar of scraping chairs. Judge Wilson sat in his chair and nodded toward the audience to sit.

"It was my intention to hear the evidence as it would have been presented and either send this case to trial or fine the suspects and send them on their way. But without proper representation my hands are tied. We will have to postpone the hearing until we have a qualified attorney to represent that band of idiots chained in the middle of the room."

Judge Wilson raised the gavel but one of Thaddeus' solicitors, Raymond Wilcox, stood to his feet.

"Pardon me, your Honor, but before we cast this hearing aside, may my colleague and I approach the bench?"

"And you're the legal representation for Thaddeus Jackson?"

"My name is Raymond Wilcox, and my friend's name is Daniel Brewer."

"I hope this has something to do with the trial."

"Yes, Your Honor, it does."

"Come ahead."

The men approached the bench.

"I hope I'm not overstepping my boundaries, but it's plain to see you're under a lot of stress, and the local attorney being out of town can't sit well."

"Get to the point, Mr. Wilcox."

"Yes," Wilcox cleared his throat. "My friend and I are both seasoned attorneys, and Mr. Brewer is willing to become a public defender for the men in chains if it would help speed things along."

"Is that right, Mr. Brewer?"

"Yes, Your Honor."

"Okay, give your information to the clerk then meet with Sheriff Blankenship to set up a time when you can meet with your clients."

The judge banged the gavel against the podium.

"Court is adjourned until ten o'clock tomorrow morning."

******

"How's Abner doing?"

Dave Price had just unlocked the heavy door between the cells and office at the jail. The stench inside the cells caused Sally Adams to gag.

"Are you alright?" Dave asked and moved quickly to catch the tray loaded with beans and cornbread as it began to wobble.

Sally nodded as she took the tray back. "Yeah, I'm okay. How do you stand it?"

"Stand what?"

"The smell."

"Oh," Dave took his time making sure the cell with only two prisoners was locked. "We don't get much of that when this door is closed.

"Well, what about the prisoners?" Sally's complexion had grown pasty as she slid a soup bowl with cornbread and beans through the bars.

"They're the ones who started the whole thing by figuring out a way to make themselves smell that a way. As far as I'm concerned, they can live with it."

"That ain't quite the way it come down, ma'am," one of the new prisoners called Sam said. "We ain't never seen or heard of those men before."

"Well, I reckon that might be true… to one degree or the other. But the thing is, me and my pards here might spend some time in the pokey, but since we didn't shoot nobody, and we ain't stole no cattle, we're better off than you folks, cause they're gonna hang all y'all."

"It's a good thing I'm not judge over you guys, cause I'd hang every one of you, just for being a pest."

Dave turned to leave the room.

"How do you figure Abner's doing, Sheriff?"

Dave paused and looked over his shoulder.

"The doctor is trying to figure out whether or not he's going to be able to save his leg."

"It's that Injun," the other rustler said with a curse.

"Yes, Manhunter did shoot Abner in the leg," Dave said with a chuckle. "But he only fired his rifle after Abner shot at him first. In fact, if you hadn't stolen Jim Larkin's cattle and killed one of his hands, and shot a member of the posse, then you wouldn't be stuck inside this cell with these smelly sidewinders."

Dave pulled the door closed to a crack.

"The way I hear it coming down is Judge Silas Williams is going to do something with these four tomorrow morning. Then, while they are on their way to prison, he's gonna try you three."

Dave closed and locked the door while Sam was trying to ask another question.

"Is that really how it's going to happen?" Sally asked.

Dave pursed his lips and stirred the fire inside the pot-bellied stove.

"Yeah," he said with a nod. "And at least two, probably three of them are going to get hung."

******

Sam's stomach growled as he shoved a spoonful of pinto beans into his mouth. They were definitely better than he expected. He took another bite of beans followed by a bite of cornbread. The beans had been cooked with diced ham, onions and a hint of garlic… pretty much like his mother used to do. It didn't take long before the bottom of the bowl came into view. Sam quickly crumbled part of his cornbread into the remaining soup and gulped that down. He scooted back on the cot wishing he had another bowl while he finished drinking his coffee.

It wasn't that he'd never been arrested before, but he'd never stolen cattle, and definitely had never pointed a gun at another human being and pulled the trigger. Actually, he'd never pointed a gun at another human being period. But who was going to believe him, while he sat inside a jail cell with a group of crass people who smelled like they were dead.

The outer cell door opened and Sheriff Price entered with the old grey-headed man everyone called Smokey, who was carrying a shotgun draped over his arm. Sam stood to his feet as they entered.

"Excuse me, Sheriff. What are my chances of getting another bowl of them beans?"

"You liked them?" Dave Price grinned.

"Yes, sir. They was quite tasty."

"I don't know. I'll ask when we get your smelly friend to the courtroom."

It was about fifteen minutes later when Dave returned with a small pot of beans and another slice of cornbread.

"Your timing is perfect. If you had waited awhile longer you would've missed out. This is all that's left."

"Much obliged, Sheriff. I was starving to death."

"You're always starving," Jason Odell said from his cot. The man had hardly eaten any of his supper.

"It doesn't look like you're hungry at all," Dave said.

"Well, let's see you get locked up next to the rotting corpse six feet away, then see how hungry you get."

"Yeah, he is irritating, isn't he?" Dave said. "Well, Cotton and Manhunter say their ready to see him, so you'll get a little fresh air for an hour or so."

"Is that so?" Cherry Michaels rose off his cot in the neighboring cell and rattled the bars.

"Gee, is that supposed to scare me?" Jason laid back on his cot smoking a cigarette and laughed.

"If they let me out of here, we'll see just how scared you are."

"Okay, children," Dave said as they unlocked Cherry Michael's cell. "They aren't going to let you out of here without Judge Silas' blessings, and that ain't likely to happen anytime soon."

"Come on out, son, and don't try no funny business," Smokey said as he cocked both hammers on the shotgun. "I've been around for a while and know how to use this here scatter-gun."

"They ain't gonna keep me very long, and we'll settle this when I get back," Cherry yelled and gave Jason an obscene gesture.

"You know something Cherry? I really hope they do. There's a real nice patch of level ground behind the jail near that old scaffold I'd love to stuff your smelly rear into."

"Come on, Cherry," Dave said and gave the man a shove. "I'd like to get a little sleep in my own bed tonight."

"Nope," Smokey said as Cherry started to turn toward Jason's cell. He shoved both barrels of the shotgun under Cherry's chin and walked him out the door.

"Huh," Jason said as he laid back on the cot. "I guess that old man does know how to use that shotgun. Oh, you might as well eat my beans and cornbread, if you want. I ain't very hungry tonight."

Chapter 25

Judge Silas Wilson held court the following day behind closed doors with Sheriff Price, Matthew Blue and several pillars of Leon society until he created a plan that served justice well. It was midafternoon when Smokey and Dave Price unlocked the cell.

"Okay, you four smelly varmints, on your feet and keep your mouths shut." Smokey kept the shotgun pointed at Cherry Michaels.

"Where are we going, Deputy?"

"You and your friends are going to see the Judge. The word is, he's gonna pass judgment on you."

"Hah!" Cherry shouted as Smokey prodded him with the shotgun. "I told ya they weren't gonna keep us very long."

Cotton and Dave herded the four men into the courtroom and kept the shotgun pointed at the prisoners with a warning. "Stand quiet and keep your traps shut unless Judge Wilson asks you something. Is that understood?"

"Yes sir. We can do that," Cherry Michaels said with a laugh.

"That rule from the judge was supposed to start before you stepped into the courtroom. One more outburst like that and I'll march all four of you right back to that cell and leave you there," Dave Price said.

Judge Wilson took his time shuffling papers and stuffing them into folders. He stuffed the last paper into a folder and folded his hands to study the men.

"Well, you certainly don't smell any better, I'll say that for you. Even after we made all four of you take baths, you're right back smelling the same, and your language hasn't improved either. I'm going to release you in a few minutes and here's what's going to happen. You're going to collect what personal items you have and leave town.

"Now, listen to me," he continued. "You are not to enter any stores or eating establishments. You are to leave Leon and never return. I need the manpower and resources to try some real lawbreakers instead of childish pranksters like you. Is that understood?"

All four men nodded.

"I do have warrants for your arrests in case you decide to show up someday. Now, collect your belongings and be gone." Judge Wilson cracked the gavel and waved at the men as if he were shooing a fly. Smokey followed behind with the shotgun as the men collected their belongings from Cotton at the back of the courtroom.

"Keep moving, boys. Don't even stop to breathe," Cotton said.

"Someone open some windows and give us some fresh air," Judge Wilson said.

A band of curious citizens had collected in front of the courthouse and several of them burst into laughter and whistles as the men left the building. Cherry Michaels grew sullen and morose when it dawned on him that they had made him out to be a joke… something to laugh at.

"All y'all keep moving. We have your horses here at the livery, all saddled and what not," Smokey said.

"Nah, that ain't right," Jason Odell said, shaking his head.

"What ain't right?"

"This might be my hoss, but the saddle belongs to Laredo."

"Well, I'll tell you what," Cotton said. "Fork your horses like they are, then switch saddles and what not when you get out of town."

Caroline was inside the livery checking on Laughing Brook when the sound of a mob caught her attention. She climbed up on the stall's railing to peer over the heads and looked directly into Cherry Michaels' face. She raised up higher and saw Thaddeus Sr. and his children leaving the hotel and heading their way. She scurried back down and elbowed her way through the crowd saying "excuse me, sorry, excuse me."

Thad Jr. broke through the crowd opposite Caroline when Cherry immediately gave him a shove and guffawed as Thad caught his balance by catching hold of Caroline to steady himself.

"There he goes again, hiding behind a woman's skirts. Why don't you admit it, fancy-pants. You're afraid of me."

"Go fetch the sheriff at the courthouse," Smokey told one of the men as he leveled his shotgun at Cherry.

"You know something Cherry," Thad said as he removed his jacket. "I've had just about enough of you."

"Well, what are you gonna do about it, fancy-pants?

Thad handed his jacket to Caroline and placed his derby on her head then ducked as Cherry threw a looping right hand that caused Caroline's stomach to knot up.

Thad threw a left jab that landed on Cherry's nose and then he danced away gracefully. Cherry's face reddened as he charged after Thad, swinging wildly and catching nothing but air.

Sheriff Price burst through the line of men and women with Matthew Blue and Cotton on his heels. He took one look at Smokey and said, "What's going on here?"

"Just what you see. The first thing Cherry did was pick a fight with young Thad, and now he's getting his clock cleaned."

"I wouldn't have believed that happening. He's got forty pounds on Thad," Cotton said as he re-holstered his pistol. Cherry bellowed as he dove, hoping to pin Thad to the ground, but Thad skipped out of the way, then landed a vicious right hand that buckled Cherry's knees. He landed several more blows before Cotton stopped him.

"That's enough, son. He ain't much of a threat to anyone now.

Cherry made a grab for Cotton's pistol but Smokey whacked Cherry across the head with the butt of the shotgun.

"Why didn't you just shoot him and do the world a favor," Beverly said, her comment drawing laughter and applause.

Thaddeus Sr. scowled at his son's hand that was starting to swell and turn purple and shook his head.

"You'd better take that over to the doctor's office and have him look at it. We've got to collect and deliver a hundred head of horses fairly soon and it's just you and me, son."

"You've got to be joking," Sam said with a laugh. He was in a conversation with Dave Price and wasn't backing down. "I ain't helping that tub of lard onto his horse. He can climb onto his own horse hisself. Besides, he's the reason we're all mixed up in this mess in the first place, and I'm quitting this outfit as soon as I leave town."

Matthew grabbed the reins to Cherry's horse and placed them into Cherry's hand.

"There, the problem's solved. You can walk and lead the horse until you feel you can ride. Then, climb on your horse and just keep going."

There was a small portion of the crowd that chose to follow the four prisoners out of town and harass them as they went. Caroline almost felt like skipping as she gave Thad Jr. his jacket and derby.

"Here, don't forget these." She slipped the hat on his head and cocked it slightly. "You were quite impressive, the way you handled that big man. Where did you learn how to do that?"

"He was on the boxing team at Harvard College," Beverly said proudly.

Caroline chuckled as Thad gazed at her silently.

"You'd better do what your father suggested and have Doc Williams look at your hand. It might be broken."

"You'd best listen to her, Tex," a lanky cowboy ambled up to join them. "Please excuse the intrusion, ma'am, but I just wanted to offer my congratulations to this hunk of driftwood here." He glanced at Thad's hand and cocked his head to one side. "But I reckon offering a handshake is out of the question."

"Dad? I'd like to introduce you to… Rio, is it?"

"Yes, sir." Rio shook Thad Sr.'s hand. "Proud to make your acquaintance."

"We met Rio and his friends in El Dorado," Beverly said as she wrapped both of her arms around one of Rio's. Where are your friends, anyway."

"Arizona and that lot? I figure there around here someplace. More'n likely looking for work, same as me. We tried working on them oil rigs and none of us liked getting that dirty. Besides, I'm a cowboy, not a grease-monkey. I figure if it can't be done by horseback, it ain't worth doing. We heard a man by the name of Larkin might be looking for some drovers."

"If he isn't, I am." Thad Sr. said.

"Really? doing what?"

"Rounding up a hundred head of horses and moving them to a collection site," Matthew said.

"Build a remuda?"

"Exactly. And once they've been collected, we need to break them as best as we can."

"And what are these hosses gonna be used for? Rio took the makings out of his shirt pocket and casually rolled a smoke.

"The army, mister Rio," Thad Sr. said. "The horses have already been sold, so money's not the object. The only thing we don't have is cowboys like you to run the thing. So, how about it? Do we have a deal?"

"All four of us?"

"All four, if they will work."

"They will. For how long?"

"As long as needed. Depending on how it goes, it might be permanent."

"Come on, big guy." Caroline grabbed one of Thad's arms and tucked her arm in it. "I'm taking you to see Doc Williams. It doesn't look like you're going to go on your own."

******

Late that afternoon Thaddeus Sr. requested everyone's presence inside Zydeco's where they found Yvonne dressed in white and Thaddeus in a black suit. Yvonne's father was also dressed in a black suit. The back wall was lined with tables of food and a small white wedding cake.

"Wow! Caroline said as she turned in a slow circle. "How did they find the time to do all this?"

"You can do almost anything you want… if you have the money," Thad said with a laugh. It was Thad Sr. who tapped a spoon against the side of a wine glass to get everyone's attention.

"I met this lovely lady several years ago in New Orleans, but then lost track of her and could not find her or her father at all. But a miracle happened a few weeks ago when I walked through that door." He pointed. "I decided that night that I was not going to lose her again. So, I asked her to marry me… and she said yes."

"Now, tell the truth," Vicky said as she leaned close to Matthew's ear. "You knew about this, didn't you?"

"I had my suspicions, but what fun would it have been if I'd just told you?"

Yvonne tapped on her wine glass with a salad fork. "I too thought I'd lost him." She smiled toward Thad Jr. and Beverly. "I hope we can become close friends."

"If you can make Dad behave, we already are," Beverly said and hugged Yvonne tightly.

Yvonne grabbed Thad Sr.'s hand and held it as she smiled throughout the ceremony, performed by Pastor Billings.

Chapter 26

Beverly slept late and the bright sunlight that greeted her as she stepped on the wooded walkway in front of the hotel both blinded her and made her feel warm all over. She inhaled deeply and released it slowly. It had been a particularly bad night assisting Doctor Williams in surgery. When the doctor opened up the rustler's leg, he found the leg full of bone fragments as he suspected it might be. Then the doctor insisted she quit administering ether until the rustler came to. At that point, the surgery became the busiest room in Leon, with Cotton and Dave teaming with Dr. Williams and Judge Wilson, trying to get the man to allow the doctor to complete the operation.

"Nah, ain't happening! You ain't cutting my leg off," the man known as Abner yelled and cursed as the men insisted the operation was necessary to keep him alive Finally, after nearly two hours of pleading, Abner gave in.

"Let's go have a cup of coffee at the restaurant before we start the operation," the doctor said to Beverly. "I'm exhausted already."

They crossed the street to Zydeco's, where Yvonne poured two steaming mugs.

"Your father is looking for you. Perhaps you should tell him you are helping the doctor again tonight."

"Okay." She wrapped her fingers around the warm mug and inhaled the steam. "I will do that as soon as I finish this coffee."

Feeling useful had always made her joyful, and seeing Jack shuffle-walk around the doctor's office had filled her completely full. "You watch him closely and make him sit and rest now and then," Doctor Williams said. "And for Heaven's sake, don't let him fall. That would undo everything we've been trying to accomplish.

"Did you have anything to eat while we were waiting for Abner to make up his mind?"

"No," Beverly said and blew the steam from her cup.

"Perhaps you should eat something before we start," Doctor Williams said.

"Did you eat anything?" Beverly said over the rim of her mug.

"Don't worry about me. I learned how to eat a sandwich between operations back during the war."

Since she didn't want to hear another story about the Civil War, Beverly finished her coffee in relative silence. Besides, she had a lot of things to ponder concerning her friendship with Caroline Blue. Sometime during the operation to save Jack's life, she felt *she* needed to be the one to take care of him. Then while she was waiting in the hotel lobby before Abner's surgery, Jack had come through the door. Seeing his pale complexion, her heart went out to him.

"There you are," he said and sat beside her on the bench with red velvet padding.

"Yep, here I am. How's your arm doing?

"It's doing fine. Want to see?" He started to remove the arm from the sling.

"No, Jack! You open that wound and start it bleeding again, and the doctor will kill us both. You shouldn't even be out of bed."

They sat silently for a few minutes as the sound of a guitar and a fiddle floated through the front doors that were propped open for ventilation. Two men passed the hotel and one of them laughed.

"It's a nice night. Wanna' go for a walk?" Jack said.

"I'm sorry Jack, but the Doc's wife won't be home until sometime tomorrow afternoon. So, I'm on nurse duty. We can sit here and talk."

"Okay, what do you want to talk about?"

"Oh, I don't know. Why don't you tell me about Mr. Larkin's ranch?"

"Well, first of all, it's big, and down-right pretty. It's several thousand acres of green grass and streams."

Jack went on to describe the bunkhouses and garden area where Mrs. Larkin grew fresh vegetables. Without realizing it, Jack kept getting closer to Beverly until their lips were touching. They were snapped back into reality as Caroline walked up and stood inches from the couple, holding a mug of steaming coffee in her hand.

"Caroline! I thought you'd gone home." Jack's voice quivered as he tried to get up, but Caroline crowded him, forcing him back to the seat.

"Obviously. I doubt very much if you two would be sitting here locking lips if you knew I was still in town."

"Caroline…" Beverly started but Caroline held up her hand, cutting her off.

"You know what, Beverly? There isn't a thing you could say right now that would interest me." She turned to leave, but spun back around.

"Oh, I brought this for you, but I don't think you'd mind sharing with Jack, would you?"

She dumped the mug into Jack's lap, then pitched the empty mug to Beverly. "It belongs to Zydeco's."

Jack was still hopping and dancing around, trying to keep his clothes soaked with hot coffee away from his body.

"I've known Caroline Blue most of her life, and I do believe that is the first time I've seen her this angry," Randal Turner said as he came from behind the counter carrying a couple of towels. He gave one to Jack and began mopping the wet sofa. "Yes sir. I think I'd stay away from her for a while."

Chapter 27

Caroline walked briskly toward the livery and knocked on the office door.

"We're closed."

Smokey's gravelly voice seeped past the wooden door. Afraid she couldn't make it through one sentence without crying, she knocked again.

"I said we was closed. Come back in the morning."

"S… Smokey? I need to come in."

"Caroline?" The thud of his heavy boots hitting the wooden floor sounded as the old man rushed to unlock the door.

"Why didn't you say it was you, child? I would've let you in long ago." A light came on as he lit a lamp and the door swung open.

"How come you ain't home with your family? Did something bad happen?"

"Yes." She fell into his arms, sobbing.

"Well, tell me what happened. Did someone shoot Matt?"

She shook her head.

"Yer ma then? What happened to her? Spit it out now."

"No, nothing's wrong at the ranch. It's me. I'm the one who's broken," she said between sniffing.

"Aw, now that's too bad. Come here, child, sit yourself down and tell me about it." Smokey glanced around the room and moved a couple of boxes on the table until he found a semi-clean rag and gave it to her to use as a hanky.

"Mama said the school board decided classes would be suspended tomorrow so that the children would get to see the inside of a real trial in progress. Well, I decided to pack a few things and spend the night at the hotel in Beverly's room. I couldn't find either of them, so…"

"You couldn't find who?" Smoky said.

"Jack and Beverly!

"Oh… okay. Go ahead.

"Anyway, I just now found them, inside the hotel lobby, sitting on the red velvet bench, hugging and kissing each other."

"Naw, you don't say! Ain't you and Jack supposed to be getting married?"

"Yes!"

Smokey got up and pulled two small glasses from the cupboard and set them on the table.

"What'd they have to say 'bout themselves?"

"Nothing."

"Nothing?"

"No, they didn't say anything, Smokey. Not a word. I guess Jack doesn't want me. What's the matter with me Smokey? Why doesn't Jack want me?"

"There ain't a blooming thing wrong with you, so get that thought out of your head. What's happening is you ain't no little girl anymore. You ain't interested in playing with dolls and things. You've grown up and pretty soon, your pa's gonna be chasing young men away from that ranch with a shotgun. You mark my words."

Smoky opened several drawers before pulling a bottle of brandy from the desk then filled both glasses.

"Jack wanting that big city girl instead of you." Smokey shook his head. "If that don't add a skunk to the woodpile, I don't know what does."

The brandy burnt a trail from her lips to her stomach, and left her gasping for air.

"That's what they call *sipping liquor*. You're supposed to sip it a little at a time. Don't go telling your ma and pa about me giving you that. They'd skin me alive and nail my hide to the barn door. But I've found a small glass every now and then takes the edge off bad things."

"Thank you, Smokey. You've always been a good friend to me, as long as I can remember."

"You're welcome. There ain't a day goes by that I don't wish you were my little girl. Want me to shoot Jack's leg off to teach him a lesson?"

"Not unless there's a way to do it without you having to go to jail."

They finished their brandy and talked until Caroline started yawning.

"Okay girl, we need to figure out some sleeping arrangements. I don't reckon you wanna sleep in the hotel with that city girl, so let's see what we can come up with here." Smokey fumbled through a sea chest and came out with a folding cot and a couple of blankets. In a matter of minutes Caroline was asleep, hugging the wall farthest from the door. She woke before dawn to discover Smokey had used several saddle blankets to make a curtain between them.

Smokey's snoring sounded like a buzz saw as she crept around the room, looking for a writing tablet. She left him a note in the middle of the table, thanking him for taking her in the previous night. She also found a stale biscuit and confiscated it. She normally wouldn't fool with a saddle, but she was wearing her best dress, so she quickly tossed a blanket and saddle on Laughing Brook and led her out the back way to the livery and down the road. *Jack Caldwell and Beverly Jackson be hanged.*

She stopped at the edge of town and adjusted the cinches. Somewhere a dog barked and the creak of a door on rusty hinges squawked as she swung into the saddle. Remembering Smokey's warning about Laughing Brook's left rear hoof, she set the horse's gate at a walk. Caroline sat easy in the saddle and ate the stale biscuit as the sun peaked over the eastern hills.

Chapter 28

Beverly Jackson woke at daybreak with a feeling of foreboding. It only took a couple of seconds to remember the chaos she had caused with a simple kiss. It wasn't the kiss itself, but *who* she had kissed. She relived the entire incident down to Caroline dumping the coffee into Jack's lap.

If that wasn't bad enough, Randal Turner told her father and brother what had happened, and she had to sit and listen to one of her dad's lectures, only this one was different.

"I should lecture you on the value of a good friendship, Beverly, but I'm not. Caroline Blue has been a true friend to you and this family. Kissing her fiancé?" Thaddeus shook his head and turned away. "What were you thinking?"

If the truth were known, she wasn't thinking. That was the problem. Beverly liked that Jack Caldwell was a fine specimen of a male and she had felt a strong attraction the first time she had laid her eyes on him. And yes, she had to admit, he acted brainless at times, like the incident at the church, but that just added to his likeability. Then, at other times he could be so attentive and kind.

Beverly quickly dressed and ran a brush through her hair. She grabbed her handbag and exited the room. Caroline wouldn't listen to reason last night, but maybe she would this morning.

When Randal told her Caroline wasn't at the hotel, Beverly drifted from one building to the next, places where Caroline might be staying, but no one had seen her. But it was early and most people were still inside their houses. She was sitting on a wooden bench in front of the hotel when Yvonne waved to her from across the street and held up a steaming mug of coffee. Beverly crossed the street and took the cup from her hand.

"Thanks, I needed this."

"You're quite welcome. You still haven't found your friend?"

"No. Have you seen her?"

"Yes, I did see her, early this morning when I took the trash out."

"Where was she going?"

"I did not ask," Yvonne shrugged her shoulders. "She had her horse, so I supposed she was going for a ride."

Beverly gave Yvonne back her mug and almost ran to the livery. The old man who ran the place almost treated her with disdain and kept his comments to a few short words like "nope" or "can't say." Worst of all, he kept telling her he had no horses for rent when over half the stalls had horses in them.

"Yeah, but them are working horses, and their owners will show up pretty soon wanting to toss saddles on 'em."

Beverly turned slowly, searching in desperation for some miracle to get her out the mess she had caused.

Sitting in an empty stall by itself was Thad's horseless carriage, covered with a tarp. Beverly jerked the tarp off the shiny red paint and quickly primed the carburetor. She grabbed the engine crank and gave it a twirl.

"Hey, get away from there." Smokey yelled from where he was pitching hay. "That contraption doesn't belong to you!"

"No, it belongs to my brother and I can use it."

Smokey opened the stall gate as she twirled the crank several more times. The engine caught and started with a bang. Every horse inside the stable whinnied and ran circles inside its stall.

Beverly grinned as she climbed into the driver's seat and threw it into gear. The autocar lurched as it crossed the stable and out the gate. Smokey dove for cover as Beverly guided the auto out onto the street and turned toward Matthew Blue's ranch.

"I say good riddance and don't come back anytime soon." Smokey picked up his pitchfork and returned to the horses.

The town was wide awake now, and Beverly had to drive slower than she anticipated. She gritted her teeth as two dogs bolted toward the car, barking and snarling. It wasn't until she took the left fork in the road that she thrilled at the four-horse-power engine. She pressed the throttle all the way open and the vehicle skipped and rocked from side to side down the road.

The roadway took her down toward the creek crossing and back up. Her heart started pounding as she spied a lone female rider about a quarter-mile ahead in the middle of the road, looking back at the her. The rider walked the horse off the roadway and waited.

Beverly slowed the vehicle, feeling anxious, and prepared to stop. She brought the autocar to a complete stop and locked the brake, but Caroline turned her horse and trotted ahead.

"Caroline! Caroline! Wait a minute!"

She kept going and Beverly had to crank-start the engine again. She released the brake and drove ahead. Caroline stopped Laughing Brook just off the road and waited. Beverly stopped the vehicle but left the engine running.

"I know you don't want to talk to me, Carol, but just listen. Okay?"

"As I said last night, there's nothing you can say that I want to hear."

"Just try me. I had a sleepless night last night. I was miserable."

"Good. You should've been. Now, move."

"No, not until you hear what I have to say." Beverly grabbed the horse's reins.

"Let go of my horse, Bev."

"No, you've got to listen to me first."

"Are you really sure you want to start this now?"

Beverly shrank back, realizing her mistake. While Caroline was one of the prettiest women she had ever seen, she also had to work hard to earn and keep everything she had. Caroline was also bigger and stronger than her. She would have to rely on her wits... if she had any.

"Whatever it's going to take to get you to listen to my side."

"Your side? I didn't know girls like you had a side."

"And what's that supposed to mean?" Beverly gave Caroline a shove, and Caroline gave her one back, harder.

Caroline prepared herself as Beverly charged like a bull. She side-stepped the angry girl, tripping Beverly and landing her in the mud. Caroline hiked her dress and tucked it in at the waist to give herself more movement.

Beverly came off the ground and threw a handful of dirt and gravel into Caroline's face, then charged again. She landed a hard right fist that knocked Caroline down, and Beverly landed on top. It took about two seconds for her to realize the move was her worst yet. She grabbed a fistful of Caroline's hair only to discover she had latched onto a bobcat that hit and bit and kicked. All she could do was let go.

The two women paced around, sizing each other up. Caroline stepped in quickly, hitting Beverly with an open-handed slap that left a bruised handprint on Beverly's cheek. Beverly took a couple of stagger-steps before landing on her butt.

"Had enough, Beverly?"

The girl nodded.

"You might be able to steal my boyfriend, but I'll never let you beat me in a fight. And I don't care that we were supposed to be friends. I won't let it happen."

"I need to talk to you, Caroline. And it does matter to me that we were friends. I hope we still can be friends."

"So talk."

"I was sitting there in the hotel lobby waiting for you when Jack came in and we talked awhile. And before I realized what was happening, he kissed me."

"And you didn't kiss him back? Come on, Beverly. I'm supposed to believe that?"

"No, I did kiss him back. Wait a minute," she said as Caroline started to leave.

"Make it fast. Unlike you, I have to work for a living."

"I kissed him back because I was flattered that my best friend's fiancé found me attractive. I'm sorry."

"You are pretty, Beverly, but that doesn't excuse anything."

"You think I'm pretty? I've never thought I was pretty, but then I grew up around actors and the rich and famous, so… " Beverly shrugged. "Some of their morals were not the best. Normal people don't act that way and it doesn't excuse what I did. I'm sorry. I hope you can forgive me some day."

Caroline had her arms crossed and stood staring at the girl and tapping her foot.

"Oh, come on and get this thing started," she said, tying Laughing Brook to the back of the machine.

Beverly grinned as she jumped into the driver's seat.

Caroline climbed into the passenger seat and glared at her. "Laughing Brook is worth a whole lot more than this thing we're riding in. She's got a bruised hoof, so you're going to have to go real slow. Got it?"

"Yes ma'am." Beverly killed the engine and had to pull the crank to restart it. She released the clutch and kept the vehicle rolling at a walking pace. Caroline checked on the horse every few minutes by looking over her shoulder. They hadn't gone but a couple of miles when Caroline signaled for Beverly to stop.

"Why? What'd I do wrong?"

"It isn't something you did. Listen."

Beverly killed the engine and Both girls listened intently.

"I don't hear anything but cattle."

"That's just it. This is our property and outside of our milk cow, we raise horses, not cattle."

"Let's go see." Beverly jumped out of the car and gave the engine a couple of cranks. She walked the car down into the wash and up the other side and stopped. Not thirty yards or more away, the wash was full of cattle that were moving their way.

"Now, isn't that the most beautiful sight you've ever seen?"

Both girls jumped as Andrew Thomas walked his horse from behind a thicket of cottonwood trees.

He shook his head and laughed.

"Caroline, Caroline, Caroline. What am I supposed to do with you girls?"

"Who owns the cattle, Mister Thomas?" Caroline tried desperately to sound commanding, but wasn't sure it worked.

"Well, for the time being, I do."

"Did you get my dad's permission to move them across our land?"

"Now, there's the kicker. No, I didn't get his or anyone else's permission."

"Then you'd better get them off our land, because my dad wants the grass to feed our horses."

"Oh, I know quite well what your Indian father wants or doesn't want. But you see, this wash is a good way to move cattle in broad daylight without being seen. And better yet, it dumps into my land just north of this ranch. Once we get the cattle there, we won't bother you again for a while." He tilted his head and grinned. "No, I won't bother you and your friend very long."

Andrew motioned with his hand and two scruffy-looking cowboys joined them.

"Let me introduce you to a couple of my men. This fellow answers to Red, because of his hair. Folks call his partner Waco, 'cause that's where he hails from. They're going to be your escorts for the rest of the day. Now, I'd do what they say, because they can get rather mean when you don't."

"Why don't we just pop them and get it over? We've got cattle to move," Red said as he pulled his pistol.

"Because we will be telling the world we're still out here rustling. Better lock them in the old Soddy until I can come up with something better."

"Okay, ladies," Waco said with a laugh. "You heard the boss. Climb up into this contraption and let's go."

"Please turn my horse lose. She's lame."

"Maybe so… but the saddle ain't," Red said as he stripped Laughing Brook of her saddle and swatted the pony on the rump. The horse immediately darted toward Matthew and Vicky's ranch. He tossed the saddle into the car and grinned. "You never know when a good saddle will come in handy."

Caroline's stomach knotted as the man hooked a rope around the steering column and tied it to the pommel on his saddle. The horse he was riding pulled the vehicle with ease. The men traveled back the way Caroline and Beverly had come until they came to a small creek trickling from a sandstone hill that partially hid an old sod house with the windows boarded up.

"Alright, climb out. This is where you'll be staying until the boss decides what to do with you," Waco said as he unlocked what looked like a fairly new padlock. The hinges on the door squealed as he forced it open and pushed Caroline through the door, followed by Beverly.

The girls sat down on the cold plank floor and listened as the men glared at them.

"As pretty as they are, it seems a waste killing them both when neither of 'em have been used," Red said.

"And how do you know if they've been used or not?" Waco laughed. "Besides, I don't care one way or the other. I want the little dark-headed one myself."

"Suits me."

"Just so you'll know ahead of time, this is the only way in or out of this place, and it's been boarded up pretty tight. We'll be back to visit in a few hours." Waco laughed and gave the door a shove.

Beverly released a sob as the door squealed shut and the men drove in several nails to make sure it stayed that way.

"Oh, God, what have I done? Those men are going to take advantage of us and then kill us both." Beverly gripped Caroline's arm.

"Shhh," Caroline said as she pulled Beverly's hand away. "Crying isn't going to help us at all."

The girls crowded one of the windows and watched through the cracks in the boards as the men tossed several tumbleweeds and some brush on the car to hide it from view, then rode away.

"I don't want to die, Caroline. What are we going to do?"

"I don't want to die either, but like I said, crying and moaning won't help."

Caroline hiked up her dress and pulled the knife from its sheath.

"I don't suppose you have one of these?"

Beverly shook her head slowly as she watched a beam of sunshine from the boarded window dance across the blade.

"No, I don't. But I've got to get me one of those."

"Now's when we prepare for battle," Caroline said as she began tapping on boards attached to the sod walls. "Why don't you look for some sort of weapon while I look for an exit."

In a few minutes Beverly found a rusty knife and a broken shovel handle. She sat on the floor and ripped several strands from her petticoat then she tied the knife to the shovel handle.

Caroline found a loose board behind the rusty bed frame and tugged on it several times until it gave away with a crack. "Eureka!" Caroline came up holding a broken board.

"Come here and I'll show you something."

"What is it?"

"It's our way out of here."

Beverly squatted as she stared at the hole in the wall.

"It's a hole that goes back into the hill."

"Sure it is." Caroline knelt beside her and grinned. My dad said the old trapper who built this place was eccentric and was afraid of sleeping in a one room cabin with only one door. So, he dug a way out of here. The only question is if the tunnel is still connected."

They worked together to pull off a couple more boards.

"So, do you want me to crawl to the end of the tunnel?"

"Yes, take your spear and get going, in case those men get back here sooner than they said."

Beverly grabbed the handle and rusty knife and crawled into the blackness. She could hear Caroline scratching and scraping behind her. Beverly inched her way deeper into the blackness until something happened behind her and the sliver of light disappeared. She moved slowly forward but couldn't hear anything from Caroline. She took a few more crawling steps until panic set in.

I don't hear Caroline…they came back early and they're gonna rape her and kill her. Next, they're coming after me.

Suddenly, Beverly couldn't breathe and could feel herself slipping away.

"God no!" She screamed as she tried turning back. "Caroline!!"

"Ow! Stop it!"

Beverly felt someone tugging on her spear and was certain it was Red or his partner. She charged ahead throwing punches.

"I said stop it." Two strong arms grabbed her by the shoulders and shook her violently. "Now, knock it off!"

"Caroline?"

"Of course it's me. Who did you think it was?"

"I don't know. I thought it was those men. I couldn't see anything."

"Are you afraid of the dark?" Caroline said with a chuckle.

"No… I don't think I am."

Caroline couldn't help giggling.

"It's not funny!"

"No, I don't guess it is. You'd better keep crawling or they *will* catch up to us. And watch that danged spear of yours. You poke me with it again and I'll take it away from you."

About ten minutes later Beverly poked her head through a shoulder-wide opening covered with sticks and brush. She quickly turned back and offered Caroline a helping hand. As they stepped out, both girls breathed deeply. Beverly took a good look at Caroline and burst out laughing. Caroline took one look at her mud-covered arms and dress and grinned.

"I'm guessing I look pretty much like you."

"I'm sure you do." Beverly climbed onto a rotting log and looked around.

"Which way is Thad's car?"

"Almost directly below us." Caroline pointed.

Beverly craned her neck to see what Caroline was pointing at and quickly ducked back down.

"What's wrong?" Caroline said.

"They're back," she said in a hoarse whisper.

"Where?" Caroline peeked over the rotting log to see the two men riding up the center of the wash.

"What are we going to do?"

"The only thing we *can* do. Sit right here and see what they're going to do."

Chapter 29

The courtroom had turned into a three-ring circus with Daniel Brewer strutting around and quoting points of law, doing his best to prove to the courtroom he was a force to deal with. Judge Wilson finally stopped the young attorney to remind him it was just a hearing, to decide if the men caught with stolen cattle by the river should go to trial. Matthew found the whole thing humorous until Brewer referred to Caroline as being raised by Indians and someone who was responsible for starting several brawls in the street. That was when Matthew got out of his chair and left the courtroom.

"Hey, Matt." Dave Price followed Matthew out the door.

Matthew stopped and glared at him.

"Where are you going? I think Cotton's going to call you to the stand right after the bag of wind decides to sit down and shut up."

"Nah, you don't need me in there. I might get het up and say or do something we'll all be sorry for."

"Okay, I can see your point. But where's Caroline and her friend Beverly? Cotton wants them both on the stand."

"I don't know where they are. That fancy red putt-putt machine of Thad's was gone when I passed the livery. I figure they took off in it somewhere. I'll ask Smokey if he's seen them."

Matthew heard Dave yell as he strolled rapidly toward the livery stable. "We need both of them girls, Matt. You might remind them of that."

Matthew found Smokey sitting at the table inside the livery office eating eggs with biscuits and gravy.

"Grab yerself a plate and sit down, Matt. I made plenty of gravy and biscuits, and it will only take a minute to fry up a couple of eggs."

"Much obliged." Matt split a couple of biscuits and held the plate while Smokey fried the eggs. He sat across the table from Smokey and took a couple of bites.

"Mmm, it's good."

"Shore it is. Ain't nothing like down home cooking." Smokey took another bite. "What's going on at the courthouse. I figured you to be involved one way or the other."

"I was… or am, I guess. But I had to get out of there before I bagged myself a lawyer."

Smokey laughed and wiped a little dribble of gravy from his beard.

"There was a time not too long ago when you and me wouldn't have needed a judge or a courthouse to settle our differences. We'd have taken care of it ourselves out on the prairie with our guns and some good rope. Your folks know that more'n the rest of us."

Matthew nodded his assent as he took another bite.

"I hate to ask this, but have you seen Caroline around anywhere?"

"Caroline? Shore, I seen her. She spent the night right over there on the cot. Now, don't go turning sour on me, Matt. She was all hurt and busted up inside and needed someone to talk to and I'm sort of like a grandpa to her. She caught that city girl hugging and kissing with Jack Caldwell over at the hotel."

"City girl? You mean Beverly Jackson? I thought they were friends."

"Shore you did. Most everyone in Leon thought they was friends, the way they hung around together. But I guess she was only friends long enough to steal Jack Caldwell out from beneath Caroline's feet. When she'd gotten most of the hurt inside of her talked out, I made up that old army cot right where it's sitting, and that's where she slept. She was gone when I woke this morning. That note is what she left me." Smokey pointed at the folded paper with his gravy-laden fork.

"If you're looking to find her, you might try your own house. I'm surprised you two didn't pass each other on the way into town."

"I had a couple of things to do before I got here this morning." Matthew rose from the table and shook Smokey's hand.

"My pleasure, Matt. And, just so you can't say I didn't warn you, you might have to break up a cat fight before you get home. That city girl came looking for her and, when she found out that Caroline had her horse, she fetched her brother's horseless carriage outa the back stall and took after her."

"Well, let's pray I get there before they declare war. Beverly has those long fingernails and knows how to use them."

"Yeah, let's pray it don't happen. But I figure Caroline can handle herself in most any scrap if she wants to."

Matthew ran back to the courthouse and almost drug Vicky out the door. After telling her what he'd learned from Smokey, he re-saddled the pinto and galloped out of town. The horse made quick time of the trip and Matthew dismounted in his own front yard without seeing anything of Caroline or Beverly, either one.

He checked the house to see if she had left a note explaining what was going on, but found nothing. He stripped the saddle from the pinto and tossed it on the back of Mark's horse when Tippy started barking.

"The dog might be old and crippled, but he still has the heart of a warrior." Shadow grinned from where he sat on his pony.

"It's good to know Shadow hasn't lost the magic of silence. I didn't hear you come. What brings you this far from the reservation?"

"Food. It's always the same thing, Manhunter."

"Vicky isn't here now to cook for you, and I'm kind of busy. But you're welcome to get down and eat anything you find. If you wait awhile, I'll be back shortly."

"We know you are busy, Manhunter." Shadow laughed loudly. "You are looking for the princess and her friend, are you not?"

"Yes, I am." Matthew gave the cinches a tug. "Do you know where she is?"

"Yes. She and her friend are being chased by two white men with guns. The men have horses, while the princess and her friend are on foot. Something happened to the red machine that needs no horses and the men buried it under some weeds. The princess and her friend got away for a while, but it won't last long. I left Low Dog there to watch."

Matthew shoved the Sharps rifle into the sheath and swung into the saddle.

"Where are they?"

"Right here… on your own property. Living with the white people so long has made you soft, Manhunter. Come; Rain in The Face and I will show you."

"Wait, I forgot something."

Matthew dashed into the house and returned with the longbow and a quiver of arrows.

"Where'd you get such a large bow, Manhunter?" Shadow said as he turned his pony away from Matthew's house.

"It was a gift from Caroline when she returned from school. The bow is very old and has a lot of magic. I'll tell you more after we save the girls.

Chapter 30

Red and Waco rode up in front of the soddy and dismounted. Caroline could hear the men as they pounded on the boards they'd used securing the door, then the screeching of rusty hinges as they pushed the door open.

"They ain't here," Red hollered.

"What do you mean *they ain't here*?" Waco yelled back.

"Exactly what I said. They ain't here. Come take a look."

What followed was a plethora of cursing and throwing things around the room.

"I don't care much about the girls, myself," Waco said after they had finally settled down. "What I *do* care about is them telling some lawman what we've been doing and me getting tossed in some jail somewhere or getting hung. So, come on. If they got out of here, we should be able to figure out *how* they got out."

"Well, I kinda figure they're still around here somewhere," Red said and kicked a broken chair.

"How's that?"

"They ain't got no horses and that red thing they rode on getting here is still parked outside."

"Good thinking. Come on, help me have a look-see."

******

Caroline and Beverly crouched low in the weeds and watched the men. She tugged on Beverly's arm and pulled them both lower.

"Here's where we have to be brave. They'll find out how we escaped sooner or later, then they'll be up here."

"What are we going to do? I don't want them touching me." Beverly looked like a frightened little girl as several tears wet her cheeks.

"Well, I don't want them touching me either, but I'm not giving up without a fight. Look," Caroline pointed toward a grove of trees. "That's where my house is. I'm thinking we'll take off running and make a beeline for the trees."

"I don't run too good in this dress." Beverly shook her head slowly.

"Then take it off." Caroline unbuttoned her own skirt and petticoats and let them fall.

"We can't do that, Caroline. People will see us in our unmentionables." Beverly's voice was a hoarse whisper.

"I'll run through the middle of town buck-naked if it'll save me from what those men say they want to do to us. Make up your mind Beverly. They're coming now!"

Beverly peeked over the crest of the hill and saw the men taking their time climbing the hill toward them. She quickly jerked her dress off, popping the buttons, and grabbed her make-shift spear and with a "Let's go," darted downhill toward the distant trees. Caroline grabbed two fist-sized rocks and took out after her.

Chapter 31

Matthew pulled the black and white sorrel to a halt on the top of the small hill as the girls came into view. Neither girl had her dress on and they were running in their underwear. Two men on horseback were circling and closing in on them in an effort to bring their chase to an end. If it were Caroline herself, he wouldn't be so worried. The girl had grown up on the ranch and had spent her entire life working hard, or wrestling with him and her brother. It was Matthew himself who taught her how to fight with a knife and had given her the knife attached to her calf. But Thaddeus' daughter had never experienced any of the advantages Caroline had and even now was tiring and slowing them up.

Shadow and Rain in The Face stopped their mounts beside Matthew and watched.

"The race is about over, Manhunter. What are you planning to do?"

"I might kill me a couple of white men. You don't have to watch, if it is going to bother you."

"No, you know better than that." Shadow grinned as he injected a round into the chamber of his Henry rifle. "Three Horns said Caroline was a Comanche princess. I don't plan on just watching."

That was when the men crested the hill in front of the girls. Beverly stopped running and bent over, clutching her side and trying to catch her breath. Caroline looked at Beverly before letting out a war-whoop and charged. She threw one of the rocks at a dead-run and hit Red in the mouth. Blood splattered on the saddle as Red fell from the horse.

"You little… "

Waco's oath was cut short as Beverly charged, throwing her spear that bounced off his chest. Waco grabbed for his rifle but dropped it as he cried out and bent over. An arrow had imbedded itself almost to the feathers near Waco's right collar bone. Beverly made an effort to hide behind Caroline as Caroline's father and three Indians dismounted. A very large black Indian took one look at them and burst out laughing.

"I see you had a time of it, Princess."

"I don't know if I would call it that, Shadow, but I can't describe what it felt like to see you gentlemen show up."

Low Dog joined them and handed the girls their dresses. Caroline thanked him in Comanche and immediately slipped into her petticoat and skirt. Beverly was slower until Shadow assured her none of the men present would see anything.

They walked back to the Soddy and the girls drove Thad's horseless carriage to the ranch.

Mark was feeding the horses when they rolled into the yard. Caroline shook a fist at him as he burst into laughter.

"I'm warning you, Mark Blue. I'll break every bone in your body if you don't stop it now."

He did stop when his father rode in with the prisoners being flanked by Shadow and the braves. Vicky came from the house to help the girls and saw the men. She took one hesitant step toward them when Matthew held up his hand.

"Don't come any closer, Vicky. These men are dangerous. I'm going to go with Shadow to deliver them to Dave. After the girls have cleaned up and you're finished with the chores, you should come to town with the girls. Dave and Cotton will need to talk to them."

"What's going to happen?"

"Well, for one thing, Caroline and I both are going to be called as witnesses. What else," Matthew shrugged, "I can't really say."

******

The busy little town became deathly quiet as Matthew led the procession down the street toward the jail. The presence of four Comanche braves with two white prisoners caused a low rumble to roll through the crowd. The war with the Comanche had been a long, vicious one that most people still remembered, and many held grudges.

Andrew Thomas did a little nervous dance on the walkway in front of the bank as Matthew and the Indians dismounted in front of the sheriff's office. Red and Waco were supposed to be excellent shots with either a Winchester or a handgun, and were the last persons Andrew Thomas expected to see this afternoon, especially covered in their own blood. He allowed himself to be swallowed by the crowd until he headed directly toward his own store where he locked the door and pulled the shades. This whole mess should have been cleaned up long ago, but it was too late to worry about it now. With Red and Waco in jail, his name was going to be linked with the rustlers in a matter of hours. He'd have to leave Leon now.

He grabbed a suitcase and crammed it full of clothes. Then he emptied the register and cashbox into a pillowcase and crammed it into a second pillow case. He stood in the middle of the room looking around. Everything had started to go wrong when he had to shoot Bobby Sorenson. The stupid kid wasn't even supposed to be on that part of the Larkin Ranch. But then he started threatening to tell Jim Larkin about the rustling like he was dealing with a bunch of school kids.

He left both suitcases lying on the bed when someone started pounding on the door. He checked the loads in his Colt and held his breath as the pounding continued. The knocking finally died down and he heard whoever it was walk away. Andrew released his breath and sheathed his gun. He went out the back door and walked quickly to the livery. He could see Smokey inside the hay loft, staring at the circus in front of the sheriff's office.

"What's happening at the jail, Andrew? Got any idea?"

"Only that Matthew and some Indians brought in a couple of men all buggered up. That's all I know."

Smokey climbed down the ladder and spit on the pile of muck on the ground.

"Must be connected somehow to the rustling. What can I do for you?"

"Oh, I've got to leave town on some business, so I'll need to rent the buggy. I shouldn't be gone for more than two or three days."

"Sure, it's right in here. Y'all going very far?"

"No, I'm heading to El Dorado. Trying to expand," Andrew said with a crooked smile. "You know me, Smokey."

"It's getting kind of late to be heading to El Dorado. It'll get dark before you get halfway."

"Yeah, but I know a rancher just a little farther out than Matthew Blue's place where I usually sleep. He's got three daughters that are worth the trip by themselves. You know the type."

"Yep, reckon I do." Smokey walked two buggy-trained horses backward to the buggy. "Well, if you ever find the secret to making lots of money and finding a good woman to spend it, let me know."

"I'll do that," Andrew said with a laugh.

With the team of fresh horses attached to the buggy, Andrew drove to the rear of his shop and tossed the suitcases into the back seat. He turned the buggy at the first wide spot in the street and pointed it toward El Dorado. Shaking the reins, he glanced over his shoulder as the buggy caused the crowd to shrink back. The team was well-fed and rested, and ate the miles beneath them quickly. Andrew allowed the horses to race down the road as he formulated a plan inside his head. He would ditch the rig and horses when he reached El Dorado. But from then on, he was going to rely on modern modes of transportation.

He would buy a ticket on one of the trains and head south. In his mind that would be a lot better than going north or west, because almost everyone wanted to go west, and he was certain Dave and Cotton would spend quite a bit of time looking for him there.

He would change his identity and maybe even grow a beard and change his name. He felt a little giddy at the thought that he might even find a good-looking woman and get married, have some children.

He was jolted from his daydreaming when the buggy jerked sideways and bounced violently with the sound of splintering wood. It was all Andrew could do to keep from being ejected from the buggy.

"Whoa," he yelled and brought the horses to a halt. There was a trail of broken spokes and buggy parts from a protruding granite boulder that Andrew had hit with the right rear wheel as he made the turn way too tight. The buggy now sat in the middle of the road, leaning to one side with the metal wheel ring perched on one broken spoke.

Andrew cursed loudly and kicked the broken wheel, causing the metal rim to slip and land on his foot. He hopped around on one foot like a chicken, cursing, then sat in the buggy rubbing his wounded foot and trying to come up with another plan. As it was, he was stuck about two miles from Leon, and a long eight miles from El Dorado. One thing for sure, he couldn't walk back into Leon carrying a bag of money without getting questioned about the murders and rustling.

He unhitched the horses and whacked them both on the rump, sending them back to Leon. What he needed was a gasoline-powered buggy like Thaddeus' boy had. Then he could go almost anywhere.

Chapter 32

Both girls sat quietly in the back of the wagon and rocked with the motion as Vicky guided the wagon toward Leon. Mark had begged her to let him drive Thad's horseless carriage, but to no avail.

"No, you've never ridden in such a contraption and it has to cost more than you earn in an entire year. If you wrecked or damaged it, we'd never be able to pay him off. Besides," she said as she climbed into the wagon, "you can bet he's going to want to check that horseless carriage from top to bottom to make sure it's okay to ride in." The closest he could get to driving the car was to hook a tow rope from the wagon to Thad's vehicle then sit in the driver's seat and apply the break when they needed to stop.

They drew a small crowd when they reached the outskirts of town and were followed to the sheriff's office. Several people shouted questions to them, but Cotton and Matthew escorted them inside.

"We'll tell you all the particulars when we get it sorted out," Dave yelled, then he took Vicky and the children to his own house where Susan already had dinner cooked.

Caroline and Beverly sat side by side inside the sheriff's office while Raymond Wilcox took notes on the proceedings. Cotton grew red-faced with anger when Caroline described the conversation between the two men where they described which girl they wanted. She then went on to describe what they had planned on doing with them after they had used them.

"I hate to ask this question, but I need to," Cotton said. "Did those men touch either of you in an inappropriate manner?"

"No." Caroline shook her head.

"Beverly, what about you?"

"No, but they wanted to."

"Are you sure? I heard that both of you were missing some drastic clothing."

"That was my idea, Uncle Harvey. We took off the long skirts so we could run."

Cotton gave Matthew a questioning look and Matthew tilted his head and shrugged.

"Have you ever tried running in a dress like they wear?"

"No, and I don't ever plan on it." Cotton turned back to the girls. "So, they didn't touch either one of you?"

"No, they sure tried but Caroline wouldn't let them," Beverly said.

"What do you mean?"

"What I mean is, she knocked Red's teeth out with a rock and was getting ready to charge Waco when Mr. Blue and those Indians shot him."

"In all your conversation with them, they didn't happen to mention who they're working for, did they? Matthew asked the question as he rolled a cigarette.

"They didn't have to. Beverly and I almost ran into him with Thad's autocar," Caroline said.

"Well, don't make us guess. Who is it?"

"It's Andrew Thomas, Dad."

"Andrew?"

"Yeah," Beverly said. "And he's the one who ordered those men to take us somewhere and kill us."

"Isn't he having some sort of trouble right now? Cotton said.

"Yeah, he rented one of Smokey's buggies to head to El Dorado and the horses came back by themselves. I was going to ride out that way and see if I could locate him, but this came up instead," Dave said.

"Maybe one of us should go to his store and see if he showed up," Cotton said.

"What about the girls?"

"You ladies might not like it, but we need to make sure you're safe until this whole thing is over. I want you both to stick together and stay at the hotel. That means *you don't go anywhere without the bodyguard, period.* Got that? I'll appoint a bodyguard to be with you twenty-four hours a day."

******

Andrew Thomas sat on a boulder shielded by several cottonwoods, and studied the city from a distance. It didn't take much imagination to understand what was going on. The large crowd gathered in front of the sheriff's office was angry and milling around. While he was seated on the rock, he watched as Smokey left town with two extra horses and a spare wheel and returned with the broken buggy. Andrew cursed himself for not being more careful. He would have been close to El Dorado by now, instead of sitting on a cold, hard rock.

He watched as Smokey unhooked the horses and disappeared toward the sheriff's office.

Andrew made himself more comfortable by stripping leaves and creating a make-shift bed to lay on. Eventually, the boredom of watching the crowd got to him and he dozed off, only to be awakened by the cold, damp air. The town looked like a ghost town. He worked his way down the boulder and toward the livery. He heard the howling of a coyote somewhere in the distance followed by the barking of a dog at the opposite end of town. Andrew stopped and stared at the livery's office as Smokey's snoring grew louder. *You've gotta do something about that snoring, Bud.* That was when he decided to use Smokey's snoring to his own advantage. He would move around inside the livery, and hold still when he was quiet…which was seldom.

Andrew first planned on taking one of the older buggies, but the sight of Thaddeus' horseless carriage parked inside an empty stall was just too much to bypass. He opened the stall door and placed the suitcases in the rear luggage compartment. He released the brake and smiled as the autocar rolled easily out of the stall door and into the street, until he cranked the steering wheel hard to the right and was facing an uphill grade. It wasn't much of a grade as grades go, but enough to make pushing an autocar a challenge. Andrew grunted as he used his shoulder against the door frame. The vehicle rolled slowly, inch by inch, but at least it was moving. He finally crested the incline and set the break before leaning against the autocar, trying to catch his breath.

Chapter 33

"I'll take the first watch," Matthew volunteered.

"Are you sure? You've been at it all day and half the night," Cotton said.

"Yeah, but I won't get any sleep with all those kids thrown together either."

"Alright. Just don't forget I offered." Cotton pounded on the door to Beverly's hotel room and it opened immediately.

"See?" Cotton almost yelled. "That's exactly what I've been saying is going to happen all along."

"What are you talking about, Uncle Harvey? What'd we do wrong?"

"You opened the door."

"Well, what was I supposed to do?" A crease appeared between Caroline's eyebrows. "You were talking loud enough to raise the dead."

"Well, just so you know, your pa's volunteered to be your bodyguard 'til early morning. Then Dave's going to take over. So, you two take it easy on them. Okay?"

"We will. So, can we get some sleep now?"

"Sure, go right on and go to sleep."

Beverly burst into giggles as Caroline closed and latched the door.

"Is he always like this?"

"Who? Uncle Harvey?"

"Yes."

Caroline pursed her lips in thought, then burst into laughter.

"Yeah, pretty much. But I don't know who I'd rather have on my side when things get dicey, except maybe my dad or Dave Price."

The girls crawled into bed and Beverly fell fast asleep. It was Caroline who decided she needed to use the chamber pot before sleeping. She tossed the blanket back and crawled around on all fours, peering under the bed but could not locate the pot. She finally decided to use the public chamber down the hall. Caroline cracked open the door and peered out into the hallway. It looked as though her father was sleeping in a chair leaned against the wall.

I'm going to have to have a talk with my dad after this is over, she whispered to herself. She stepped into the carpeted hallway in her bare feet and closed the door.

"You don't need to be so quiet," Matthew said without opening his eyes. "But I recommend wearing a robe over your nightgown. Otherwise, others might get a peek at parts of you they shouldn't. "Go on, I promise not to peek," he added as she started to reopen the door.

Caroline ran to the chamber and stepped inside. Feeling relieved, she started back toward Beverly's room when she glanced out the window. Someone was opening the gate to the livery. Caroline stood fixed as a lone figure disappeared back into the livery, then reappeared pushing Thad's horseless carriage.

"Hey, Dad! You'd better take a look at this."

"What's going on?" Matthew joined her side.

"I don't know, but as quiet as he's being, I don't figure Smokey knows he's being robbed."

"You get back into your room and lock the door."

She watched him disappear down the stairway before closing and locking the door. *God, please take care of my daddy.*

******

Andrew cursed loudly as Matthew Blue came from the hotel and stared right at him. Andrew jerked his pistol from the holster and fired. He then jumped into the car and released the brake. The autocar started rolling away from the city.

Andrew's heart almost stopped as he looked over his left shoulder and saw Matthew Blue a matter of yards behind. He swore as he ground the gears and released the clutch. The vehicle lurched with a loud bang as the motor started and he pulled away from Matthew, who was reaching for the rear door. Andrew pulled his pistol from the holster and fired again.

******

"What's going on?"

Caroline glanced over her shoulder to see Beverly sitting up in the middle of the bed.

"Someone's trying to steal Thad's horseless carriage."

"No!" Beverly said and dashed toward the door and tried to open it.

"My dad said to keep the door locked."

"But it isn't your dad's autocar someone's stealing. Come on, Caroline I need to see this."

Caroline released her hold on the door and ran to the window with Beverly crowding in with her. Whoever it was suddenly turned the vehicle to the right.

"What's he doing?" Beverly said.

"I think he's trying to get it out of town. The other way he'll have to go completely through town."

The thief was at the crest of the climb and paused to catch his breath when Matthew stepped out of the shadow. The thief brandished a pistol and pulled the trigger. Caroline screamed and bolted toward the stairs, but Beverly caught her arm.

"Your dad's okay! He's chasing after the guy.

"Come look. Besides," she added as Caroline looked over her head, we can't go down there like this."

"What's going on?" Thad Jr. left the door to his room standing open and joined them at the window.

"What's going on is, someone's stealing your carriage," Caroline said.

"Her daddy's down there now, trying to keep it from happening."

A second shot caused Caroline to jump, just before the thief got the carriage to roll forward. With a grinding of gears and a loud backfire, the vehicle picked up speed and rolled away.

"No!" Thad Jr. bellowed, tand dashed to his bedroom to get dressed.

"Son, hold on there. Let the law handle this," Thaddeus Sr. said. He had come from his room with a pair of pants on under his night shirt.

"We've already done that, Dad, and look where that's gotten us."

"That's *my* dad down there trying to save your precious autocar," Caroline yelled and turned back toward the window.

"She's right, son. You need to be a little more gracious.

"Well, I'm going down and try to help Caroline's daddy." Beverly turned away toward her hotel room.

"It doesn't look like we're needed," Thaddeus Sr. said with a chuckle. "Here," he stepped back to let Beverly have the window. "Take a look."

The first person she saw was Smokey standing in the middle of the street holding a shotgun. Matthew was talking to him and motioning with his hands. Cotton and Dave joined them, as well as Yvonne, holding a shiny pistol in her hand.

"Well, we have a small army down there," Thaddeus said and ran his fingers through his hair.

"Yeah, but where is my autocar?"

"Right there." Caroline stepped back and pointed at the window. "It went down the Mill Road."

Chapter 34

Andrew Thomas laughed loudly as the car pulled away from Matthew's grip. He knew the Mill Road well enough to know it was constantly being maintained and had few problems. He shoved the throttle wide open and held it there. The carriage flew past the first dip in the road and gained more speed as the road to El Dorado came into view. He slowed to make the turn and the carriage coughed, then leveled out.

"Come on, baby. Just get me to El Dorado and after that you can roll over and die, for all I care. That cough almost seemed like an omen as the carriage coughed several more times, then died.

Andrew yelled curses at the top of his lungs and beat on the steering wheel with both fists. His knowledge of autocars had come from washing and cleaning the horseless carriage owned by the warden's wife in Yuma, Arizona. It was a place he swore he'd never return to, even if he had to put the bullet into his brain himself.

He climbed out of the rig and cranked the engine over several times; he got one little cough, but it wouldn't start. He tried several more times before giving up, so he grabbed the money suitcase and started walking. He rounded a bend in the road and stopped. Three Comanche Indians mounted on magnificent horses were blocking the road and they didn't look like they were in a good mood. He turned around as if he was heading toward Leon and stopped. Matthew Blue was blocking the road.

They walked their horses toward him. Glancing around, he saw that the biggest of them carried a decorated lance that was pointed toward Andrew.

"What is in the case, white man?"

"It's mine. You can't have it."

The Indians roared with laughter.

"Who's going to take what's inside the case is up to me, and you don't have any say in the matter," Matthew said. "Now, I'll repeat Shadow's question one more time. What is in the case?"

"I already told you. It belongs to me and you can't have it."

Andrew had no more than gotten the words out of his mouth when Shadow charged his horse toward Andrew and whacked him across the head with the blunt end of the lance.

"Nice way to end an argument," Matthew said as he opened the suitcase.

"How much do you think there is?" Shadow asked as they crowded around.

"More than enough to buy that store of his. Do you want to help me deliver our thief and the money to Dave Price?"

"Sure. I haven't made the sheriff sweat in a while."

******

Given the time of day when they arrived in town, and the fact that everyone seemed to be starving, Dave Price talked Yvonne into opening Zydeco's one last time to feed Shadow and his braves.

"You might not agree with it when you first bite into it," Dave said.

"Why not? Is she a bad cook?"

"Nothing's wrong with it. It's Cajun cooking," Cotton said. "It can get hot sometimes, but I like it myself."

"Then, lock our friend in one of the cells and let's go," Shadow said.

******

The sight of a Comanche War Chief and two of his braves entering an eating establishment drew a small crowd in front of Zydeco's. Someone called out, "I ain't eating there anymore! There's no telling what you'd catch eating off those plates, even if they was washed real good." Others chimed in with their agreement.

Thaddeus Sr. stepped outside and closed the door.

"Gentlemen, please give me your attention for a minute. First of all, no one can catch anything from a plate or fork that has been cleaned properly, which is what is going to happen here. Secondly, Zydeco's will be closing its doors to business today. Mr. La Rouge is ill… not from eating with Indians, but because his heart is giving out. So, we would appreciate your cooperation. Please move along while we feed the men who captured your rustler and recovered a large amount of money, which we believe came from selling the stolen cattle."

Yvonne did most of the cooking, following her father's directions, then started to wait tables. Caroline had somehow slipped past Cotton's guards. She handed Rose to her mother and tied an apron around her waist.

"Don't worry," she said, when Yvonne told her to sit down. "I've had quite a bit of practice waiting tables while I was away at school."

The Comanches ate everything Caroline sat in front of them and sopped their plates.

Chapter 35

Cherry Michaels dismounted and tied his horse to the corral fence then motioned for Jason Odell to follow.

"What are we doing here, Cherry? That old judge told us we ain't welcome here, and he'd lock us all up if we ever showed up in Leon again."

"What's the matter, Jason? Ya turning yeller on me?"

"No, I ain't turning yeller. I'm just trying to stay out of jail."

"Ah, I heard that old man ain't a real judge, he's a pig farmer."

"Yeah, and I heard old Roy Bean ran a trading post until he held court. I also heard those people he hung are still dead." Jason Odell spit into the dusty street and wiped his face on his shirt sleeve.

"Well, are you in with me or not?" Cherry stomped around in a tight circle.

"In on what? You want me to bust into that boy's hotel room so you can beat up on him again?"

"That's what I've been saying, ain't it?"

"You already had your chance, Cherry, and that kid beat the crap out of you. What makes you think it will turn out any different?"

Jason Odell climbed back into the saddle and nudged his horse away from the corral.

"I'll tell you what I'll do, Cherry. I'll wait for you by the fork in the road. If you beat the kid up, you can meet me there. By my calculations, I figure he'll whup you again and that sheriff will lock you back in that same cell. Yep, that's what I figure will happen. I'll put on some coffee and wait until about ten o'clock, then I'm gone."

"Well, if you're not willing to back your saddle pard on a deal like this, then I figure we ain't pards no more."

"Nah, I'll wait by the campfire just like I said, Cherry, so if you escape outa Leon without having a gut full of buckshot, swing by there and I'll have a hot cup of coffee waiting.

"Well, good riddance to ya!" Cherry yelled as Jason trotted his horse up the middle of the street and out of town. Cherry tossed the stirrup over the pommel to adjust the cinch when the distinct sound of someone cocking the hammers on a shotgun made his heart jump.

"There ain't no need for you to go to that trouble, son. I want you to drop your pistol and your hunting knife right where you are, then back away until I tell you to stop."

"And what if I don't want to go?"

"Then I get to kill you, right where you're standing."

"It's best to listen to him, boy." Sheriff Dave Price came from the shadows of the livery and pointed his .45 at him. "So, what's it going to be? You going to surrender nice and quiet-like, or does Smokey get to shoot you with the shotgun?"

Cherry made a whimpering sound as he looked around.

"So, whadda ya think, Sheriff? Want me to bore him now? This ol' gun might wake some folks, but it'll sure rid Leon of some undesirables."

"Oh, I don't know, Smokey. If you shoot him, then we'll have to clean his innards off everything. There's gotta be a better way of doing things."

Dave pulled a new ax handle from an opened barrel and whacked Cherry hard across the top of his head.

"Huh," Smokey said as he took a bite off a plug of tobacco. "I reckon that'll do it, except now we'll have to carry his fat rear end to jail."

"Yeah, and I forgot what he smelled like."

"How about we just drag him?" Smokey said and spit. "It ain't that far to your office."

"No, it isn't. Grab an arm and let's get it done."

Chapter 36

Dave Price rapped the gavel loudly and raised his voice. "Here ye, hear ye! The City of Leon Municipal Court is now in session, the honorable Judge Silas Wilson presiding. All rise." The noise inside the small courtroom quieted as Judge Wilson seated himself and adjusted his glasses.

"You may be seated."

Judge Silas began thumbing through a folder and taking his time as Dave leaned next to Cotton's ear and whispered.

"His wife told me that the sow he was worried about is doing fine. This may be a long day today."

"Sheriff Blankenship, bring our first case up front please."

"Yes, Your Honor." Cotton nodded toward Smokey and waited until he was in position with his shotgun before nudging Cherry Michaels with his boot.

"I really don't know what to call this one, but it concerns our stinking prisoner, Cherry Michaels, and his friend, Jason Odell.

Judge Wilson read through the charges quickly before removing his glasses to stare at Jason.

"It says here they had to ride out of town a good mile to fetch you in here today. Is there a reason for that?"

"Sure. Cherry said he wanted to collect a debt some fella owed him, so I went with him. Then, I find out what the debt is. He figures the boy owes him, because he lost face when the boy beat the stuffings out of him. So, I left."

"So, you left?"

"Yes, sir, I left."

"Sheriff Price? Is what this man says the truth?"

"Yes, your Honor. When we came on him, he had a nice camp built and was drinking a cup of coffee, and even offered us one."

"Okay, Mr. Odell, since you were not part of Mr. Michaels' plot to break into Thaddeus Jackson's hotel room again and do him bodily harm, you don't need to be here. You're free to go."

"I am?"

"Yes, and I advise you to leave Leon and not come back. There are enough people around here that have been harmed by Mr. Michaels one way or the other; I'm surprised that someone hasn't put a bullet in him."

"Yes, Your Honor. I will certainly do that."

They watched as Jason Odell collected his personal items and left the building. Matthew escorted him to the livery, where he saddled his horse and shook Matthew's hand.

"Tell everyone thanks and I'm sorry we caused so much trouble."

"You're welcome. And I hear there's still a couple of ranches in Texas looking to hire good, hard-working and honest cowboys. It might be worth checking into.”

******

“Okay Cherry. It’s time for you to stand before the judge. Up and at it,” Cotton said, but Cherry sat without moving a muscle.

“Maybe you didn’t hear Sheriff Blankenship when he told you to stand.” Judge Wilson said as he shifted in his chair. “Let me say it for him. I am sentencing you to ninety days on a road crew…”

“Wait, you can’t do that!”

“A hundred and twenty days!” Judge Wilson banged the gavel loudly and pointed toward Cherry. “Want to make it a hundred and fifty days, or maybe two-hundred and fifty?” He used the gavel as a pointer as he talked.

“This isn’t some little game we’re playing here. What I say goes around here and up to now, we’ve kind of played along with you, but no more. And every time you say or do something, it’s going to add more time to your sentence. Do you understand me?”

Cherry glared at Silas with his mouth hanging open and not saying a word, so Cotton rapped him on top of the head with his pistol.

“Ow! That hurts.”

“You give the judge a civil answer when he asks you a question.”

“Now, do you understand what I’ve said?” Judge Wilson said.

“Yes,” Cherry said while rubbing his head.

Evidently, you have trouble understanding a direct order. When we turned you loose a couple of days ago, it was with the stipulation that you were supposed to leave Leon and not come back. What happened? We found you trying to break into Thaddeus Jackson's hotel room. You said you were going to," Judge Wilson held up a court document and read it, "settle the score between you and Thaddeus. Is that right?"

"That's what it says, don't it?"

"Okay," Judge Wilson grabbed his fountain pen and signed a page and stamped it with a rubber stamp. "Breaking and entering and assault are still against the law. Sheriff Price, take this file and meet with Deputy Robarts. I've already talked to him over the telephone, and he'll be here sometime tomorrow and take him off your hands."

Judge Wilson turned back to Cherry Michaels.

"And, you are going to work for the state of Kansas breaking rocks and building roadways until your debt is paid, and don't ever enter Leon again. If you do, I am giving Matthew Blue permission to shoot you on sight. This case is closed and the court is adjourned for one hour."

Judge Wilson whacked the desk loudly. Matthew followed the judge into the back room.

"Excuse me, Your Honor, but since when are we licensing people to shoot another person?"

"We're not, but he's so stupid he'll never figure it out."

Chapter 37

"You are the filthiest man I've ever seen," Andrew Thomas growled as Dave Price locked the grimy man in the next cell. Cherry's response was to give Andrew an obscene motion as he plopped on the cot.

"Don't let it worry you, Andy. The judge is going to start your trial in about fifteen minutes. That'll require you being present at the courthouse."

"I don't know why." Andrew paced back and forth inside his cell. "That money inside my suitcase *is* mine. I worked for it, and I've already told everyone this when that Indian friend of yours joined those other Indians."

"Well, yeah, and they caught you trying to run off with everything. You even busted up one of Smokey's carriages doing it," Dave chuckled.

"Let's face it, Andy. They caught you red-handed, trying to run off with the money you got from selling stolen cattle." Jesse Roberts snickered as he crushed his cigarette butt under the heel of his boot.

"I don't know what you're talking about."

"Ya don't? Well, then you don't have anything to worry about, do you?" Jesse lay on his back laughing.

"What do you think about that, Sam? Old Andrew says he ain't guilty of doing anything wrong."

"Sounds like he's telling a big whopper to me," Sam said with a belly-laugh. "I was standing right there when he pulled the trigger and killed that boy."

"That's sorta the way I remember things coming down too," Jesse said as he fished the makings from his shirt pocket to roll another smoke.

"No, you're just trying to scare me. In fact, I know Silas Wilson, and that pig farmer is so old and feeble it's a wonder he's even able to hold court."

"Think so?" Sam said. "You was in that courtroom with me, Jesse. What'd you think of him?"

"I think Andy's in for a big surprise. I didn't see or hear anything that'd make me think the old man's touched." Jesse snickered as he lit his cigarette.

"Ah, neither of you know a thing. I've gotten myself out of jams a lot worse than this before." Beads of sweat appeared on Andrew's forehead.

"Maybe you have," Sam said. "But I hear from the old man with the shotgun that the judge told him he's planning to invite you to an air dance."

Andrew Thomas sat on the edge of his cot and covered his face with both hands as he leaned forward. He had witnessed several hangings while he was in Yuma, and believed the term *air dance* fit about as well as anything he had heard, especially when they hauled the victim up slowly. Ralph McMann was one of the unlucky ones. He had killed a dealer who he swore was cheating him in a card game. But in a quick trial he was found guilty. Poor devil was hung the very next day. His drop was way too short, and Ralph kicked and jerked as his body swung back and forth in open space. The prison officials had chosen to make the prisoners stand and watch until they were sure Ralph McMann was dead.

The whole thing was ghastly. Even now, he could see Ralph's body rocking in the hot Yuma wind and hear the creaking of the rope against dry wood.

The rattle of keys turning in the door caused him to look up.

"Come on Thomas, it's your turn to face the judge," Dave Price said as he unlocked the cell door. Andrew paused for just a second, pondering whether or not to chance it. But he saw Smokey just beyond the wooden door holding his ten-gage shotgun.

No, not today, Andrew. If it was the sheriff by himself, yeah... maybe so. But adding Smokey and the shotgun, not today.

Chapter 38

The afternoon sun was beginning to wane as Dave and Smokey escorted Andrew from the jail to the courthouse. People left the stores and restaurants to watch as they passed. Two obviously intoxicated men who Andrew didn't know pointed toward him and laughed. Mary Turner stood on the plank walkway next to the Bank of Leon with tears streaming down both cheeks. The sight of her made him yearn a little. There was a time when he thought about taking her with him, but if something went wrong, he'd have to abandon her somewhere, and home with her family might be the best.

Manhunter and Albert Meeks joined them as they reached the courthouse. Dave and Smokey ushered Andrew inside, where Cotton was waiting. He was also armed with a short-barreled carriage gun.

"Come on in, and sit yourself in that chair," Judge Wilson said as he shuffled a stack of papers.

"I'm not guilty, Your Honor. They've got the wrong man."

Andrew pulled back and Dave gave him a shove that caused him to bump into the table the judge was sitting at.

"That's not what we're here for. Sit down." He picked up a coffee mug, stared at the inside then set it back down. Matthew grabbed the mug and handed it to someone outside.

"Then what are we here for?"

"We're here to decide if there's enough evidence linking you to the rustling we've been plagued with, and with the murder of Robert Sorenson and attempted murder of Jack Caldwell. There are also several witnesses who say you gave orders to have Caroline Blue and her friend, Beverly Jackson, murdered."

"Well, none of that's true. It's all circumstantial."

"Then, which one is it, Mr. Thomas? Is what I just said not true, or is it circumstantial?"

"I don't know! All I know is I didn't do any of those things!"

Judge Wilson heaved a deep sigh as he stuffed the paperwork into its folder. He folded his hands and glared at Andrew as Yvonne entered the room and placed a mug of fresh coffee in front of the judge. She then disappeared back outside.

"Thank you, young lady. I need that."

The judge took a large swallow of the coffee, then glared at Andrew a few seconds longer.

"Tell me, Mr. Thomas. Do you have an attorney?"

"No, Your Honor, I don't."

"Then, the court will appoint one for you. It might take a day or two, but whoever it is will be competent. Court is adjourned until further notice." Judge Wilson smacked the gavel against the table and stood to finish off his coffee.

"What about me?" Andrew Thomas tried to stand but Cotton shoved him back to his seat.

"What about you, Mr. Thomas?"

"Where am I supposed to sleep? I hope it's not inside the jail with those putrid-smelling prisoners."

"Well, I guess you need to brace up, because that is exactly where I'm ordering you to spend the weekend.

"But I never did… "

"Yes, we all know how you've been arrested and misunderstood, but the jailhouse is the best I can do for now." Judge Wilson set the empty mug on the table and headed toward the door.

"As far as the evidence goes, with the fact that most of the men you hired are willing to testify against you, I'd say there's ample evidence for a trial.

"I'll let you gentlemen know the dates as soon as I find an attorney to represent Mr. Thomas."

They opened the door and the crowd began bombarding Judge Wilson with questions that Andrew couldn't understand as the door was quickly shut.

"Sorry about that, Andy. But we have to protect you as well as ourselves," Dave said.

"But we know all of them, don't we?"

"Most of them, yeah." Dave nodded. "But I've seen a few fresh faces around town today. Nothing like a good murder trial to stir up the cockroaches."

Chapter 39

Mary Turner threw herself across the bed and wailed into the pillow. Randal stood in the doorway to her bedroom and snickered.

"You know, I believe the best thing you could do for yourself and everyone involved is just forget about him."

"That's because you're not in love with him!"

"True," Randal grinned as he bobbed his head. "And I've never had half the town talking behind my back either."

"Randal, leave your sister alone." Their mother's voice came from the small living room where she was trying to feed Mr. Turner a bowl of hot oatmeal. Randal had no idea what was keeping the old man alive when half of the gruel ran down his face, instead of staying in his mouth.

"She's acting like a child, Ma. And I warned her about getting involved with Andrew Thomas in the first place!" He yelled the last part toward Mary's bedroom.

"Yes, but love can make a young woman do things and act in strange ways sometimes."

"They are talking about hanging him," Mary howled. "Besides, you do so!"

"Do so what? I have no idea what you're talking about."

"You do so! Beverly bats her eyes at you and you do anything to cater to her whims and wishes."

"Beverly Jackson?" Randal burst into laughter.

"My dear sister, Beverly Jackson is a spoiled fourteen-year-old child, whose father happens to be filthy rich."

"People still talk."

"So, let them. If you look at the books, you'll see where I charged her father dearly for all the sandwiches and cookies and baths she orders. Since I am twenty-seven years old, I have no intention of getting myself involved with a spoiled brat, which is what you're acting like. Grow up, Mary."

"You grow up! You'd marry Beverly Jackson in a minute and you know it."

Randal snickered.

"It wouldn't be so bad if I did marry her. She's not too bad to look at, and look at the money I would marry into; it would ease the pain of putting up with her. Either way, whatever I decided to do would be a whole lot better than spending ten seconds with Andrew Thomas."

"Ahhgg!" Mary shoved her face in her pillow and howled.

"Randal, please do what I asked and leave your sister alone," Mrs. Turner pleaded.

"I've got to get back to the hotel anyway. You might want to give her a good talking to Mom. People are starting to talk, but you and I have to live here."

Mary lay across the bed whimpering, for what seemed like an eternity after Randal had closed the front door. She finally got up from the bed and wiped her eyes and blew her nose. She rummaged through her night stand and pulled out a nickel-plated Smith and Wesson .38 caliber pistol that had belonged to her father before he had the stroke. Mary had kept it hidden next to her bed for protection. Wasn't helping save Andrew the same thing? Protecting someone you loved? She checked the chambers and they were still loaded.

Mary took her time applying some makeup to make herself look halfway presentable. Placing the gun into a deep pocket in her dress, she checked on her mother and father before stepping out into the street with no idea how she was going to get the pistol into Andrew's hands, only that he had asked for one.

******

"But if I give you dad's gun, you'll kill someone trying to get away," she argued.

"No, no, no!" Andrew frowned. I'll just use it getting out of town. Then I'll wait a few months, find a place for us to stay and I'll come back for you."

"Really? You'll come back for me?"

"Of course, I'll come back. Like I said, Mary, I need you."

It was while she was leaving the jail after her fifteen minutes had expired that Sheriff Price glared at her.

"I don't know what he's cooking up for you to get involved in, but take my advice and forget it."

"He's not *cooking* up anything, Sheriff."

"Listen to me Mary. This is a murder trial. They treat things a little different during murder trials, and it's a good way to get yourself shot and killed. Just remember that." Mary didn't have a reason she could think of, but she left the jail without trying to pass the pistol Andrew.

Chapter 40

George Pollock was still visiting his brother who had been injured in the farming accident, so Daniel Brewer was installed as Andrew Thomas's attorney.

Then Doctor Williams found Abner dead. "As close as I can figure, he had a weak heart," Doctor Williams said over a mug of hot coffee.

"There's nothing else you can think of?" Judge Wilson asked.

"No, not that I can think of. The operation on his leg was textbook, as Beverly Jackson could testify. There was no reason for him to die."

"I've known big, strong men who just up and died when they lost and arm or a leg," Cotton said. "It was kinda common during the war."

"One more thing— I don't have a last name for him. Anyone here know one?" Judge Wilson asked.

"Nope," Cotton said, shaking his head.

"Me, neither," Dr. Williams said. "I'd like one for the death certificate.

"Well, let's all check our sources and if anyone comes up with one besides Abner, let the rest of us know. Or else, his mama won't get the news Jr. won't be returning home for a visit."

Judge Wilson stood and gulped the last of his coffee.

"Don't forget, court's at nine in the morning."

Chapter 41

"What does he want to see me about, Dad?" Caroline asked as the two of them climbed the steps to the courthouse.

"My guess is he's going to ask you to take over the court recorder's job for a couple of days while Edith Griffith is in bed with the flu." Matthew held the door open for his daughter.

"I don't know about me being a recorder," she said with a nervous laugh. "I've never done this before."

"Evidently, he thinks you can."

Matthew rapped several times on the judge's chamber door.

"Come in."

Matthew held the office door for her as they entered.

"You wanted to see me Judge?"

"Yes, I need to ask a huge favor. I suppose he told you Edith Griffith is in bed with a bout of flu. I was on the verge of postponing the trial date until Edith is feeling better. But your dad showed me a letter you wrote to him while you were away at school and I must say that school doesn't seem to be wasted on you, young lady. Most people around here can't spell correctly and you can't read what they were trying to write anyway."

"But I'm a witness. Can a recorder be a witness?"

"I don't know, but I'm sure it's happened at one time or the other."

"Who's going to record the proceedings when I'm called to the stand?"

"Perhaps Edith will get over the flu and be able to take over by then. If not, we'll ask your mother to be the recorder until you are dismissed. Will you do it?"

"I guess so, if you're sure it won't get you into trouble."

******

"Here ye, hear ye! Court is now in session, the honorable Silas Wilson presiding. All rise." The acting bailiff, Sheriff David Price, rapped the gavel loudly as Silas took his place behind the podium. The courtroom had once again taken on the atmosphere of a circus. Caroline Blue was seated in the recorder's chair and was offered a job with The Walnut Valley Times in El Dorado before the day was finished. The Leon Vindicator had hired an artist to draw pictures of what was taking place inside the room. The saloon keeper was collecting bets and giving odds on Andrew Thomas' conviction. The blacksmith was taking bets on whether or not Mary Turner would attempt to rescue Andrew from the gallows. No one knew what was really true and what wasn't. Matthew was glad it would be up to Judge Wilson and the members of the jury to sort things out.

When it came time for opening statements, Daniel Brewer paced back and forth in front of the jury, assuring them that he was set to prove the case against his client was circumstantial at best, and should be tossed out of court.

Cotton, on the other hand, claimed the evidence was anything but circumstantial, and said he would prove Andrew Thomas was guilty, not only of rustling, but cold-blooded murder and several counts of attempted murder. To their credit, the reporters inside the courtroom described Judge Silas Wilson as being a tough no-nonsense judge who seized control of the trial and refused to let go. Silas banned one man from the courtroom because he would not be quiet while testimony was being given, and would not let him back inside.

The trial seemed to fall apart on day three. The prosecution presented several witnesses who said they had seen Andrew Thomas shoot Robert Sorenson point blank in the chest when Robert caught them stealing James Larkin's cattle.

Daniel Brewer countered that the evidence was second and third hand, collected outside the jurisdiction of the Leon court system, and since there was no way of proving how accurate the evidence was, it should be dismissed.

That was when Cotton invited him to step outside and settle things right then and there.

"There's no need to lose our tempers, Mr. Blankenship," Daniel Brewer said with a smirk. "I'm just stating the obvious. You're making a statement based on something told to you by a criminal facing a life sentence."

"No, you were questioning the honesty of my statement. I've been in the law business for almost forty years, and I've never told anything concerning any case I've investigated except the truth, period."

"Really? Come on, Mr. Blankenship, everyone tells a fib once in a while."

Cotton turned toward Judge Wilson and almost yelled, "Objection, Your Honor. The defense is endeavoring to paint every one inside this courtroom as liars that can't be trusted."

Silas turned toward Daniel Brewer with a half-grin. "Well, what about that, Mr. Brewer? Are you trying to put a suspicion of doubt on the witnesses the prosecution is presenting?"

"Yes, Your Honor, I am. It's part of my job. I can't help it if the testimony and witnesses Mr. Blankenship presents are so weak. It won't stand inside the courtroom."

Judge Silas nodded slowly as he glared at the two men.

"Okay, I'd hoped for a nice peaceful trial, but it doesn't look as though we're going to get one. I want to see both of you inside my office now to get this straightened out. And Mr. Blue? I'd like you to be there also as sort of a witness and a referee." He whacked the gavel loudly and left the room.

Smokey ambled to where Daniel Brewer was collecting his papers and leaned in close to the lawyer.

"If it was me, I'd change my attitude and be careful what I'd say, especially when it comes to asking them Indians what they saw."

"Oh, and why is that, Smokey?"

"Because the worst thing for an Injun to do is tell a lie. Now, the way you're going, you're gonna get one of them Comanches in that witness chair and call him a liar." Smokey bobbed his head. "You just might lose a fistful of that blond hair."

Daniel Brewer stood staring at Smokey as the man walked away. It was David Price's voice that caught his attention.

"Hey, Daniel! They're waiting for you."

He squeezed past several members of the jury who had congregated in front of the judge's door and were talking. He ignored their questions and slipped into the judge's chamber.

"There you are," Judge Wilson said. "I was about to send someone after you."

"I'm sorry, Your Honor, I had a rather pleasant visit from Smokey, in which he told me not to call one of the Comanches a liar. He said I might lose my scalp if I do."

"Really?" Judge Silas grinned and looked at Matthew. "You know anything about that, Matthew?"

"No, but it sounds like good advice."

"Which brings us back to what's been going on inside the courtroom. Anyone care to comment on it?"

Judge Wilson started packing his pipe from a tobacco tin on the desk. Both men sat silently as the judge lit his pipe and blew clouds of smoke toward the ceiling.

"No comment? That's too bad. I was hoping that we might learn something from two distinguished men like you. So, I'm going to tell you both something that's going to happen as of right now. I don't care who or what started the whole thing, and I don't want to hear about it. We're going to go back to the courtroom in a few minutes, and you two are going to join us and conduct yourselves like true professional men of the law.

Now, if you can't do that, I'll replace either one or the both of you, it doesn't make me much difference. Do you understand me, Daniel?"

He waited until he received a single nod of the head.

"How about you, Harvey. Do you understand and agree with my assessment?"

"Of course I do."

"Okay, let us go finish what we started."

Cotton led the procession to the courtroom, which caused a mad scramble for the best seats as the men took their positions.

"Here ye, hear ye! Court is now in session, the honorable Silas Wilson presiding. All rise." Dave whacked the gavel and stepped back. Judge Wilson seated himself and scanned the audience for a few seconds before pointing toward a man seated directly behind Andrew Thomas.

"You sir, may leave my courtroom now. We're having enough trouble with this case and we don't need to compete with you talking through the presentation of evidence."

The man scowled but marched back out the door.

"Now, where were we, Miss Blue?"

"Excuse me," she said as she cleared her throat. "The prosecution presented several witnesses who said they had seen Andrew Thomas shoot Robert Sorenson at point-blank range, when Robert caught them stealing James Larkin's cattle.

"Daniel Brewer countered that the evidence was second and third hand, collected outside the jurisdiction of the Leon court system, and since there was no way of proving how accurate the evidence was, it should be dismissed.

"That was when former sheriff, Harvey Blankenship, invited Daniel Brewer to step outside so they could settle things.

"Mr. Brewer said there was no need to lose their tempers. Mr. Brewer contended he was just stating the obvious. He also contended the prosecution was making a statement based on something told by a criminal facing a life sentence."

"At which point Mr. Brewer admitted the defense was trying to cast doubt on the integrity of the prosecution.

"That is when you called a recess, Your Honor."

"Thank you, Miss Blue. It doesn't sound like we accomplished a lot when you hear it read back to you, does it? Now, I would like to proceed further, but only if we can treat each other with honesty and respect. So, no personal attacks, and no fancy big-city courtroom antics. Do both sides agree?"

He waited until he received a *yes* from both sides.

"Good. We've already wasted several days just trying to get this trial started." Judge Wilson closed his file and scanned the audience. "I'm stating the obvious here. The members of the jury are not to discuss the proceedings with other members of the jury until the final deliberation, nor with citizens of Leon. Court is dismissed until 9:00 a.m., Monday, and hopefully we'll get something accomplished."

He whacked the gavel and retreated to the Judge's chamber.

Come on, Andy," Dave Price said as he took the prisoner by the arm. "Your room is cleaned, ready and waiting for you."

"Don't gloat too much, Sheriff. I'm not hung yet."

"That's true, but you're not a free man either."

Chapter 42

Caroline's lace-up shoes made a soft thumping sound as she hurried down the walkway. It was almost twelve-thirty Sunday noon, and as far as she knew, Edith Griffith was better but still feeling poorly, so Caroline would still be the court recorder tomorrow morning. "Might as well do like your Pa says and spend the night here with Alice and me," Cotton said. Caroline allowed that would make Monday morning easier, but it also meant doubling up on the chores around the ranch. Then, just like today, there was always something she might forget. Today it was her carpet bag that was stuffed under the backseat of the wagon. She would have most certainly let her mother and father drive home with it if it hadn't been for her brother asking her where it was. It contained all her extra clothing and toiletries. That would not have worked at all.

She stopped in front of Cotton and Alice's house and began fiddling with the gate latch when a *pock, pock, pock* sounded in the direction she had just come.

Thad must be going to take his car for a drive, she thought. Turning her attention back to the gate, she had just gotten the latch opened when the shiny red autocar turned off the road and rolled to a stop about eight feet from where Caroline stood.

"Where are you headed?" Thad put the car in neutral and locked the brake. "Here," he jumped out of the car and took hold of the carpetbag. "Let me give you a hand."

"I can get it," Caroline protested.

"I know you can, Caroline. You're beautiful and strong, and capable of most things. But I was hoping to do something nice for you."

"Oh." She released the bag and Thad escorted her onto the porch and into the house. Cotton and his wife, Alice, were seated at the table with Caroline's family eating fried chicken.

"Oh, there you are," Alice said as she scooted away. "Caroline? Grab another plate from the cupboard and a coffee cup for Mr. Jackson."

"Ah, nothing for me, ma'am. I just finished eating. I actually came by to see if I might take Caroline for a drive in the car? I don't believe she's ever ridden in it."

"You forgot something, Thad," Caroline said with a laugh.

"And what's that?"

"It's customary for the boy to ask the *girl* if she would like to go for a ride, before asking her parents."

"You're right," Thad said with a laugh. "How stupid of me. Would you like to go for a ride with me in the Duryea?"

"Actually, I *have* ridden in it. Remember? When Beverly was driving and the rustlers caught us?"

"Yes, you're right again." Thad rubbed his chin as his cheeks turned pink. "I guess you wouldn't care to join me then."

"Yes, I would love to join you, Thaddeus. Just let me wrap a piece of chicken and grab a different bonnet and I'll be ready to go."

"Where are you planning to take her? You realize she's been on nearly every strip of ground around here," Matthew said and took a sip of coffee.

"I really don't know. I saw an old farmhouse east of here that looked abandoned the other day. I thought it looked interesting."

"I think he means the old Hanley place," Cotton said as he repacked his pipe.

"That's a nice farm," Alice said with a nod of her head. "What would you do with a ranch like that, Thad?"

"You can't have it," Caroline said as she came from the spare bedroom. She had on a different bonnet with a scarf to hold it on her head.

"Really? Why not?"

"Because I've always wanted it. I used to play with my dolls there when my dad was working nearby. It's *my* house," Caroline said with a giggle. "I'm ready now."

"Let's go then."

Thad opened the door then looked back at Vicky and grinned. "I'll have her back way before dark."

******

Thad drove directly to the abandoned farmhouse and parked on what had once been someone's garden. He stood back and watched Caroline as she walked slowly around the house in a wide circle eating her chicken. She tossed the bone into a clump of weeds and wiped her hands and mouth on the towel.

"Would you like to go inside?" Thad asked as he climbed the steps to the front door.

"If you can get the door opened.

"I can try." Thadd worked the door handle several times and the hinges squealed loudly as he pushed the door open.

Caroline slipped inside and stood in the living room, turning slowly in a tight circle.

"How many acres are attached to this place?" Thad asked.

"I think around a hundred, but I'm not really sure."

"Why hasn't anyone snatched it up, instead of letting it decay?"

Caroline chuckled as she looked at him. "I can't really say. It could be the rumors that Hanley murdered his wife and son and they're buried here somewhere. Or, maybe the stories of ghosts flying around here at night."

"Do you believe in the tales?"

"No. I believe what Smokey said," Caroline said as she peered inside a cupboard.

"What did Smokey say?"

"That the Hanleys packed up and went back east after the locust infestation, just like a lot of people did."

"That makes sense," Thad said with a laugh.

"That's what I thought." Caroline opened and closed several cupboards and looked inside.

"I actually believe this place could be restored, with a couple of good carpenters and painters."

"I've always thought so, but it would be expensive." Caroline dusted her hands on the towel she was holding.

"This place has a lot of good memories for you, doesn't it?" Thad moved closer to her.

"Yes," she said opened one more cabinet and pulled out a small box that contained a handful of pebbles."

"What do you have there?" Thad asked as he looked over her shoulder.

"The treasury, Mr. Jackson."

She opened one of his hands and emptied the contents into it, then leaned closer to blow the dust from stones.

"It's a fortune, and I was going to do a ton of great things with the money the bank was going to give me for the gems." She paused to grin at him. "You think I'm being silly, don't you?"

"No, Caroline Blue. Would you like me to tell you what I think?"

"Yes." She nodded slowly.

Thadd poured the pebbles back into the box, then brushed a wayward strand of blond hair away from Caroline's cheek and tucked it behind her ear.

"I see a little girl who played with her dolls in this living room. She took time collecting a fortune and hid it well, so no one could steal it from her."

Thad allowed his fingers to gently caress her cheek as he leaned closer. Caroline caught her breath as he brushed her lips with his a couple of times before leaning in to kiss her softly. Caroline slipped her arms around his neck and kissed him back.

"I hate to say this, but we'd better be heading back, before they come hunting us."

"Yes," Caroline whispered against his ear.

Chapter 43

The town seemed to settle into a weekend routine designed for Leon, Kansas. Pastor Billings once again proved he was a masterful wordsmith behind the pulpit, and had half a dozen people praying at the altar by the time he was finished.

Not a word about the trial or the guilt or innocence of any of the prisoners was mentioned at either the restaurant nor the coffee shop when they opened around noon. When Monday finally rolled around, everyone arrived early and argued over which seats were still available. Most of the audience had quieted by the time Judge Silas Wilson appeared from his chamber and grinned at the somber group.

"I must congratulate this audience. It seems you have taken my words of admonishment to heart. Now, if we can just keep it that way, we'll have both a fair and speedy trial.

"Excuse me, Your Honor, but we have a request." Harvey handed the judge a slip of paper.

Judge Wilson read the note a couple of times before nodding. "Who is Mary Turner?"

"Right here, sir." The young woman dressed in black, with red puffy eyes, rose to her feet.

"Please, come forward."

She took her time, worming her way to the aisle and then to where Judge Wilson sat.

"It says here that you want the right to visit Andrew Thomas while he's in custody. Is that correct?"

"Yes, Your Honor."

"May I ask why? Were you dating him, or something?"

"Yes. Maybe not so much in public, but we did see each other privately as much as possible."

"You must have kept your relationship a secret," Judge Wilson said as he thumbed through the stack of papers on the podium. I don't find your name mentioned anywhere. May I ask why? I mean most couples will want to tell everyone when they are seeing someone. Didn't you want to tell the world about your love for Mr. Thomas?"

"Yes, Your Honor." She bobbed her head up and down. She glanced around the room quickly before leaning in to talk in a hoarse whisper.

"He's the only man I've ever really been in love with, and I'm sure I'm the only woman Andrew's seeing."

"Hmmm." Judge Wilson scratched his gray beard thoughtfully. "I can see where our arresting him and locking him inside the jail might be a hindrance to your romance. Sheriff Price? I want you and Sheriff Blankenship to create a visiting schedule for this young lady to come to the jail and visit Andrew Thomas, as long as it doesn't interfere with the trial or the giving of testimony."

"May I argue against allowing such visits to take place, sir?" Dave Price said.

"You may. Why don't you want Miss Turner to visit Mr. Thomas?"

"Mr. Thomas is a flight risk. He's already tried running away twice, and I can't see where giving Mary visiting rights is going to make him change his mind." The crease between Dave's eyes grew deeper and his voice took on an edge.

"Yes, I can see where that might be a problem, so here's what we're going to do. I want you to schedule Mary Turner two fifteen-minute visits a day. One fifteen-minute visit in the morning around breakfast time, and one fifteen-minute visit in the evening, just before bedtime. They are to be supervised, and never shall Andrew Thomas and Mary Turner be left alone together."

"That's not fair!" Mary wailed. "I wanted to see him alone."

"I'm afraid that's not going to happen. You're lucky to get any visitation rights at all. You'll take the visitations and their times as set by the court or do without."

Judge Wilson smacked the podium with the gavel. "That is my final decision on the matter."

******

Mary Turner leaned against the steel bars that separated them. The judge seemed so nice that she was certain he would pass some sort of rule allowing her access to the cell and Andrew Thomas.

"Mary," Andrew said as he tugged on one of her arms through the bars. "Stand up and listen to me. We only have a few minutes before they make you leave."

"I know, and it's just not fair." Her voice broke into a wail that made Andrew's skin crawl.

"No, it's not fair, but if you fall apart on me, that old judge and the sheriff are going to hang me in just a few days. Stay with me, Mary. I need you!"

Mary's eyes lit up at the mention of him needing her, and she gripped the bars with both hands as she stood and used the bars to frame her face.

"Really? You really need me?"

"Of course I need you, silly woman." Andrew gave her a crooked smile and reached through the bars to touch her cheek. "I've always needed you."

"That's what I told my brother, but he wouldn't believe me. He said you were lying to me because you're in trouble."

"And that's about as true as they can come up with," Andrew smirked. "But if something doesn't happen really quick, they'll hang me on that old gallows out back."

"No! Don't talk like that. I'll get you out of here one way or the other."

They both turned as Dave scooted his chair in the next room.

"You about done in there?"

"No. How much time have we got?" Mary yelled.

Dave glanced at his watch and cocked his head to one side.

"My old timepiece says about five minutes."
"Thanks.

Mary reached through the bars to pull Andrew closer.

"I have my father's pistol. It's loaded," she whispered in Andrew's ear. "How do you want it?"

"How do I want it? I want it here in my hand."

"I know that, silly." Mary saw Dave looking at them so she kissed Andrew on the lips. "My question is," she slid her lips close to his ear, "how do I get it into your hand without anyone seeing?"

"Okay, I hate to break up such a tender show of affection, but time's up," Dave said as he came into the room. "Back away, Mary. You don't want to do anything that will cause you to lose visitor's rights."

Mary gave Andrew one last little peck on the lips but Andrew forced her lips open with this tongue and ran his tongue through her mouth before letting go.

"Come on, Mary," Dave said with a snicker. "You can finish that in the morning."

******

Mary stood in front of her mirror thinking about how Andrew wanted and needed her. And why not? She might be slightly overweight, but not enough for most people to notice. Besides, Andrew needed her… he told her he did. Then there was that last kiss. She had only heard or read of such things, but never, ever experienced anything close to it.

******

What took place inside the courtroom Tuesday morning stunned Mary as Harvey Blankenship presented the evidence and testimonies against Andrew Thomas in chronological order, including the abduction of Caroline and Beverly. The last witness Harvey called to the stand was Shadow, who gave a detailed account of Andrew's capture.

"He walked up to us on the road to El Dorado, then got frightened when we asked him what was in the case he was carrying. He tried to back away, but Manhunter was there. He had nowhere to go."

Mary could only recall saying "good morning" or "good afternoon" to Harvey Blankenship once or twice in all the years she had lived in Leon. But the man pacing around in front of the judge and jury was not the soft-spoken man she had said hello to. The final piece of evidence presented by the prosecution was the brand Caroline had given to Harvey. By the time Harvey had finished, she was almost convinced of Andrew's guilt herself. The courtroom was silent until he had finished.

She had to give Daniel Brewer a nod of agreement when he presented Andrew's defense, which consisted of mostly *"I don't know who shot Bobby Sorenson, but I didn't do it."*

It was late in the afternoon when the jury was sequestered in a room in the back of the courthouse to come to a verdict. Most people wandered across the street to the café to order a cup of coffee and a bite to eat. Only about half of them were waited on when Dave Price poked his head into the café to announce that the jury had returned with a verdict.

Mary sat at the edge of the chair when Judge Silas Wilson asked the foreman if the jury had reached a verdict.

"Yes, we have, Your Honor."

"Would you please read the verdict to the courtroom?"

"Yes, Your Honor. We find the defendant guilty of all charges."

That was when Mary Turner fell from her chair and Doctor Jonathan Williams had to be called to revive her.

******

Reverend Billings made his way to the front of the church and looked at the half-filled pews. Andrew Thomas had met and influenced a lot of people in his short time in Leon. It was too bad that he couldn't have used better judgment and morals.

He had just left the jail after requesting an audience with Andrew, only to be turned down three separate times by him before giving up and leaving. He felt exhausted and ill as he pulled a wooden chair forward and sat next to the podium. Vicky Blue had told him she was going to get a few women together to pray for Andrew and those involved in the trial, and asked permission to use the church. What surprised him was how many people she had collected. He placed his head in his hands and leaned over and moaned. As the Lord Himself said, it was a horrible thing for a man to lose his own soul.

Chapter 44

"So, who's going to do the hanging?" Caroline paused to wipe the sweat from her brow. She and Matthew had repaired the broken gate to the exercise pen and were mucking out stalls in an effort to catch up on chores that had been let go during the trial.

"That's one question I can't answer. You'll just have to find out when the time comes."

"Really? What does Judge Silas plan to do… draw straws?"

"No." Matthew chuckled and took a sip of water from the canteen hanging by the barn door and passed it to Caroline.

"I'm pretty sure Judge Silas is fixing to retire, and he doesn't want the last thing he does in office to be the hanging of Andrew Thomas.

"Really?" She passed the canteen back and forked a load of dirty straw into the wheel borrow. "The man sure deserves getting hung."

"Maybe so. But the judge told me he plans on hiring someone from the prison to do the hanging."

"Where? At the prison?"

"No. He says he wants it to take place here, just so somebody else pulls the lever. They've got the railroad almost repaired, so I'm guessing sometime next week, or the week after."

Caroline shivered as she tossed another pitchfork full into the wheelbarrow and grabbed the handles.

"What about Mary? What's going to happen to her?"

"I don't reckon Dave or the judge want to have anything to do with charging her with anything. She'll have a hard time showing her face around town as it is."

Matthew grabbed the handles on his wheelbarrow and followed her to the small wash they were dumping into.

"Maybe I should go talk to her," Caroline said as she dumped her load.

"Think so?"

"Yeah. It won't hurt anyway. Who knows, she might be willing to listen to some common sense coming from someone besides her own family."

"Maybe," Matthew said as he forked some dirty straw from the next stall. "You might find her at the library. That's where she spends most of her time, anyway."

"Yeah," Caroline said with a slow nod. "I was thinking the same thing. Would you mind if I took some time off tomorrow to see if I can talk to her?"

"No, not as long as we finish these stalls." Matthew scooped more dirty straw from the floor. "By the way, where is your brother? He seems to have disappeared."

Caroline snickered as she wiped more sweat from her face. "I was wondering that myself, but didn't want to say anything. I thought you'd think I was complaining."

"No, I wouldn't think that. Neither one of you are lazy. What I *would* think about your brother is he got distracted by something other than cleaning stalls.

"Huh, maybe I can use that when it's time to give Rose a bath."

"No, don't you dare," Matthew said with a laugh.

Chapter 45

Caroline left Laughing Brook in the hands of Smokey at the livery and checked herself in the cracked mirror hanging inside his office.

"That was quite a wing-ding over at the courthouse day before yesterday, wasn't it?" the old man said. "Cotton shore put on quite a show."

"Yes, Uncle Harvey did quite well. That was the first time I remember seeing him work as a prosecutor." She stopped to smile at him. "Do I look okay?"

"Depends on whose attention you're trying to nab."

Smokey grabbed a clean rag from the table and dabbed at a spot next to Caroline's left ear.

"Had yourself a little smudge but you're okay now. You'd best get moving if you're after that rich young fella from the city. I hear they're pulling out now that the trial is over."

"Thaddeus?"

"That's the one. You didn't know they were leaving?"

"No, he didn't tell me. But I actually came to town today hoping to talk to Mary Turner."

"Oh, well, then you're more than ready. That poor girl's gone through all sorts of hell lately, and I blame most of it on Andrew Thomas. A man his age going after a young impressionable woman her age? She ain't no more than a child. Feller like that needs a good horse-whipping."

"Well, for the record, I agree with you, but you'd have to be pretty quick if you're looking to buggy-whip him. I hear the prison is sending their executioner next week."

Smokey grinned and nodded his head.

"That why you're going to see Mary Turner?"

"That, and the fact that her daddy died last night. I just want her to know there's some good people in town that will help her, if she needs it."

"Yeah, I reckon you might be right at that. I always figured she was just some half-wit they hired to do a job no one else wanted."

"Smokey!" Caroline scrunched her eyebrows. "That's mean."

"Well, it's the gospel," Smokey said with a snicker. "I ain't holding nothing against her, understand. It's just that I had the impression she'd rather sit and read a book than actually talk to another human being."

"Well, I'd say I have to agree with you on that account. But we still need to let her know we're here, ready and willing to lend her a hand if she needs it."

"I reckon you might be right, young lady. But I'm thinking it might be better coming from you. I just ain't that good when it comes to saying nice, sweet things."

"Okay," Caroline smiled and patted him on the shoulder. "I guess you're right."

******

Caroline's boots gave a deep thud as her heels hit the wooden walkway. The Turners lived in a small house one block off the main street. They seemed to be a part of a group of people less fortunate than others, although both siblings worked at honest jobs while their mother had taken care of their invalid father. Now, that was all changing.

Caroline stopped to look around and make sure she was at the right house. She raised her fist to rap on the door but stopped as Randal's voice came from inside.

"It's unlocked, Caroline. Come on in."

The hinges squawked as she pushed the screen door open.

"You'll have to forgive me for not oiling that door. Time kind of gets away from you when you work twelve-hour shifts that take most of your night."

Randy was seated at the table drinking a cup of coffee and eating a biscuit slathered with butter. Outside of a blanket that was folded and lying on a worn-out sofa, the house was neat and clean.

"You are welcome to join me at the table, if you wish. The coffee's still hot and so are the biscuits, if you want one. My mother is in the back room with one of the women from the church cleaning one of the many messes my father made. You'll just have to excuse her."

"Ah, no thank you, I already had breakfast, Randy. I was actually looking for Mary. Is she around?"

"No, Mary already went to work. What do you want to see her for? To gloat over her humiliation?"

"No, and I hope no one has done that to her."

"Well, no. Not openly in public that I know of," Randy said over a bite of biscuit. "But you know what most of the town is thinking." He snickered and shoved half the biscuit into his mouth.

"No, I can only guess what the town's thinking, and does it matter?"

"Actually, yes it does matter when you have a job like mine. I'm supposed to make sure everything is in order and to make the customers' stay in Leon as pleasant and enjoyable as possible. It's kind of hard to do that when the customer is thinking *'oh, yeah. You're the one with* that *little sister, aren't you?'*"

"Now, you're just being mean and spiteful."

"Maybe, but when did she ever stop and think about her family? I'm sure mom would have appreciated a little help taking care of dad. But you actually came to see Mary, and here I am holding you up."

"Thank you, Randy. I'll talk to you later."

"You do that, Caroline. Let me know if she will actually talk to you, or toss you out of the library."

Caroline spun on her heel and headed toward the library. The sinking feeling she had while talking to Smokey had grown into a lead weight that kept pushing her down to the walkway. She had almost reached the library when one of the cowboys Thaddeus and Beverly had befriended peeled himself off the wall he was leaning against.

"Excuse me. Miss? I don't know if you remember me or not, but… "

"Sure. You are Thad's friend. Uhh…"

"Preacher. They call me preacher because my Pa's one back in Tennessee."

"Okay, Preacher, what can I do for you?"

"You can let the girl who runs the library know that I'm here, if she needs someone to talk to."

"Really? That's not what I expected and what I've been getting. Why?"

"Miss?"

"You don't really know her, do you?"

"No, Miss, I don't know her. That's why I'm hoping you will talk to her for me."

"Wow!" Caroline said with a soft laugh and grabbed his hand. "I just hope you're still around if I ever get stomped on. Come on, let's see if she will even talk to us."

Caroline started for the door but stopped and turned toward him.

"By the way, what is your for-real name?"

"I beg your pardon?"

"I don't want to call you *Preacher* every time I want to talk to you. So, what is the name your father and mother gave you when you were born?"

"Oh, it is John. John Masters."

"I'm pleased to meet you, Mr. Masters." She shook his hand and pushed the door open. John Masters held the weighted self-closing door open for Caroline and followed her inside. The place looked empty.

"Hello?"

Caroline glanced down the first three aisles with no result.

"Hello?" she said a little louder.

"Yes, what can I do for you?" Mary Turner came from behind the next aisle dabbing at her red, swollen eyes. "Go ahead. Say what you want to say, then leave me alone."

"That's not why we're here, Miss," John said as he slowly turned his hat in his hands.

"Then why are you here? I've already been called a harlot and a dozen other names… some of which I don't even know the meaning. So go ahead and get it over with."

"It's like Mr. Masters said, Mary. We're here to help you, if you will let us."

"I don't really know you. Why do you want to help me? Besides, God doesn't want me. Why should you?"

Caroline pulled Mary close and held her tight. "Oh, Mary. Where did you get such an idea? God loves you deeply."

"How do you know what God thinks about me?"

"Because, He wrote it in a book for us to read. Come and let me show you." Caroline pulled Mary to a chair and sat beside her. She then took a small Bible from her purse and opened it. She flipped a few pages and pointed toward a verse. "Right here in John chapter three and verse sixteen. It says God loves us all so much, including you Mary, that He allowed his son Jesus to die and pay for our sins."

"Why would He do that, if he knows me? My daddy used to tell me I wasn't any good and even God didn't want me. You mean he really cares about me in spite of what I've done?"

"Yes Mary, he does. My pa is a preacher, and I grew up hearing about Jesus, and all the wonderful things he does."

Mary stared at Preacher for a minute and shook her head. "I've known Caroline for years, so I can see her getting involved, because that's what she does. But you've only been in town for a few days. Why are you here?"

"Mmm, could be I got me a sister about the same age as you, who was treated pretty much the way you were. Then, the fella she was involved with went around bragging about it. I didn't cotton to it then with my sister, Holly, and I ain't cottoning to it now."

"What did you do to him?" Caroline asked.

"Nothing much. He had to learn how to eat with no teeth."

Mary gave a sad chuckle and shook her head.

"That's a nice story and thank you for sharing it with me, but I don't see how it can help me."

"Ya don't?"

"No, I don't."

"Well, I got this letter from home yesterday," John pulled a crumpled envelope from his pocket and handed it to her. "It seems my sister and ma are both pining away, hoping I'll come back home. But I'd already told a fib by telling them I'd gotten married and my wife's gonna have a baby. The thing is, I ain't got none of that… no wife, no baby… none of it."

He turned toward Caroline and shook his head.

"That's the trouble with telling a lie. You either got to own up to being a liar, or tell another lie. So, the way I see it, Miss Mary here could pack her bags and head toward Tennessee, pretending to be my wife. Then, when she figures the time is right, I'll just sort of drift away and she'll be free."

"You'll do that for me? Why?"

"Because I think you're basically a pretty nice girl who got mixed up with the wrong sort of man. We can leave you alone, come what may, or you can come with me to Tennessee. The choice is up to you."

"What happens if she doesn't want to end your so-called marriage?" Caroline asked.

"That's easy," John said with a shrug of his shoulders. "We just stay married and raise a bunch of children."

"May I think about it?"

"Take all the time you need. But I'd stir shy of Leon this afternoon and tomorrow. I hear the hangman from the prison is on his way, and I figure you don't want to be around when that happens. Come to think about it, neither do I."

John held the door open for Caroline when Mary rushed toward them, shoving the crumpled letter into his hand. "When are we leaving?" she asked.

Chapter 46

Vicky spooned large helpings of beans and rice into bowls and set them in front of everyone around the table. Mark followed her with a pan of hot cornbread. Matthew leaned over to inhale the aroma.

"Smells good, sweetie. I didn't know you knew how to cook anything like this. What's it called?"

"Red beans and rice, and I didn't know until Yvonne taught me. They serve it all the time at Zydeco's, at least they did. Since Doctor Williams ordered him to quit working, I don't know what they're going to do."

"When are you going to tell us what happened at the library today?"

"I was just waiting to get everyone together."

"We're here now," Vicky said.

"Well, mainly, I'd gone there to tell Mary most of Leon would eventually forget about her connection with Andrew Thomas. They'll put 90% of the blame on him and she'll become the poor innocent victim."

"I think Caroline's right," Matthew said

"Well, what about the part with Preacher? What happened then?"

"I'm still thinking on that part, Mom. He was waiting outside the library as if he knew I was coming. I had planned on doing most of the talking, but he took over. The next thing I know, she's agreeing to go to Tennessee with him."

"So, none of this made a difference? She's never going to change?" Matthew said with a scowl.

"No, it didn't end like that at all, Dad. They left the library and the gang that hung out with Preacher collected at Reverend Billings house and he married them."

"He what?!" Matthew almost yelled before bursting into a laugh that woke the baby. "Man, oh man. When you get the women of this town praying, anything might happen."

"God is good, isn't He?"

Vicky was still grinning when she deposited Rose into his lap.

"You woke her… so you get to feed her."

Chapter 47

The train from El Dorado had been running late, so Judge Wilson set the execution to take place at twelve o'clock noon the following day. The hangman was dressed in black from head to foot and wore a handlebar moustache. A guard, consisting of David Price, Harvey Blankenship, Albert Meeks and Smokey exited the rear door to the jail and escorted Andrew Thomas toward the gallows. Andrew stopped to look up toward the rope and started shaking violently, making it necessary for the guards to carry the man up the steps to the rope. By that time, Andrew was crying and begging for mercy. The hangman asked if he had a last request but received no reply.

When the sack was placed over his head, Andrew went into hysterics and tried fighting the guards with his hands and feet shackled.

Cotton gave the hangman a nod and he pulled the lever. The trap door opened with a loud bang, ending Andrew Thomas' life.

Mary and John Masters left town shortly after the execution.

Chapter 48

Caroline walked Laughing Brook into the yard and dismounted. Vicky was sitting on the front porch snapping green beans from the garden. Caroline stepped past her and laid the package she was carrying on the bed then returned with a second bowl. She sat beside her mother to snap beans.

"I take it the execution went without a hitch?"

"Yes," Caroline said with a sniff. "There wasn't much else that could happen, Mom. Mary did bring her father's pistol. I guess I was the only person to notice." She shrugged. "Anyway, I took it away from her and gave it to her husband. She claimed she wasn't going to do anything but hold it." She shook her head and dumped her snapped beans in the large bowl and grabbed some more. "I don't know who to believe anymore."

"Well, at least it's over and we can get some sleep now."

"Maybe you and Pop can, but I really messed things up and didn't mean to."

"Why, what happened?" Vicky set her bowl aside to listen to her daughter.

"I moved Mary where I thought the old oak tree back of the jail would block the view. But when I looked up to see if it blocked the gallows, the executioner dropped Andrew." Caroline's entire body shook as she burst into tears.

"I'll never be able to close my eyes again without seeing his body drop."

"I know, baby. I know." Vicky held Caroline in her arms, rocking her and kissing her cheeks. "I felt much the same way after I shot that man who was trying to kill us the day your birth father died. All I can say is, the nightmares really do eventually go away."

Chapter 49

"But like I've been trying to tell you, Caroline, it was a mistake," Jack Caldwell pleaded. "Why won't you believe me?"

"Why won't I believe you? The *real* question is why were you kissing Beverly Jackson when you said you loved me and wanted to marry me? I've never gotten a decent answer to that question, Jack." Caroline's blue eyes reflected the candle on the table as she shifted in her seat to glare at him.

"I just gave you one. I was sitting on the bench talking to Beverly and suddenly, she kissed me."

"Really? Beverly told me you planted the first kiss and then she joined in. Who am I supposed to believe, Jack?" Caroline laughed and took a sip of water.

Thaddeus Sr. had requested several of his new friends to meet at Zydeco's at 5:00 p.m. for a dinner before he left town. Jack Caldwell had followed Caroline and was making a pest out of himself.

"Oh, come on, Caroline," Jack said with a bite to his tone. "It was just one little kiss and really didn't mean that much."

"Oh, don't let Beverly hear you say that. She's under the impression it meant a lot. She's liable to scratch your eyes out."

Yvonne unlocked and opened the front door and Thaddeus Jackson Jr. entered the restaurant by himself. Caroline scooted away from the table and grabbed his arm.

"I'm afraid you'll have to excuse us, Jack. My date for the evening just arrived."

Jack's face flushed as he got up from the table.

"I really wish you would listen to me."

"I have been listening, Jack. You just haven't been saying anything I've wanted to hear." She tugged on Thaddeus' arm and led him toward a remote table in the corner. Thaddeus held a chair as Caroline sat down. Jack Caldwell slammed the door as he left the restaurant.

"What was that all about?"

"Oh, it's just Jack being the same old knot head he's always been."

"Like kissing my sister?" Thad chuckled as he sat next to her.

"Exactly." Caroline laughed.

"I would have thought he had taken care of that business long ago."

"One would think so."

Yvonne approached the table carrying two glasses. I'll be joining my father and sister when they get here," Thad said.

"I thought this place was closed," Caroline said.

"We are," Yvonne said, "but Thad's father wanted one last dinner party here tonight before leaving tomorrow."

"Okay, I'll wait tables for you tonight," Caroline said.

"You don't have to do that, Miss Blue," Yvonne said with a crooked grin. "It may take a little longer, but I'll get by."

"I have a feeling this place may get pretty busy tonight. Believe me," Caroline laid her hand against Yvonne's arm and grinned. "You'll appreciate the help."

They sat quietly for a couple of minutes before Caroline spoke. "Smokey told me your entire family is leaving Leon."

"Yes, that's true." Thad nodded.

"When is that taking place?"

"Early tomorrow morning. Beverly and I plan to drive the Duryea to Chicago."

"Is that safe?"

"About as safe as anything else. I mean, we could run into a wayward rustler, or get robbed by a bandit, or meet a mean Comanche along the way. But yeah, we'll feel fairly safe. And I'm glad you're here. I need to talk to you."

"Oh? About what?

Thaddeus took her left hand and kissed her fingers before slipping a diamond on her fourth finger.

"After being around you these past few weeks, I realize I can make it without you, but I honestly don't want to. So, Caroline Blue, will you marry me?"

Caroline covered her mouth and choked back a sob.

"I was wondering how I was going to make it without you." She threw her arms around his neck and kissed him.

"Of course, I'd love to marry you, Thaddeus… but I can't."

"You can't? At the risk of sounding like Jack, why not?"

"Well, you live in Chicago with your family, and I live on a small ranch outside of Leon, Kansas. My parents sacrificed a lot to send me to school, Thad, and the same goes for you and your parents. I'm so sorry, but I can't simply move away and leave them alone."

Thad stared at her for a long minute before a smile crept across his face.

"Oh, the old *where are we going to live,* question?"

Caroline nodded as tears trickled down her cheeks.

"I'm sorry for not mentioning it earlier, but my father has most of that all worked out already; we just need to sit down and discuss it with him. From what I understand, he's moving most of his business to Leon so Yvonne can stay close to her father. He's asked her to co-write a cookbook of her dad's recipes with the intention of opening several restaurants. He wants me to help your father expand his horse and cattle business, which I know nothing about, by the way."

Thad heaved a deep sigh. "He's going to drive you crazy by the time it's all worked out. He'll want to know…"

Caroline grabbed his face in both hands and, with a crooked grin, touched her lips to his.

"Sometimes, Thaddeus Jackson the Second, you really do talk too much.

End

Author's Notes

Regarding the horseless carriage:

As early as 1770, Frenchman Nicolas Cugnot invented a steam-powered cart for moving military equipment, which was big, very heavy and cumbersome. It didn't go over too well.

In 1885, two different cars with gasoline engines were invented by Gottlieb Daimler and Karl Benz. They were the first successful attempts at the gasoline engine.

In 1895 the Duryea brothers won a race (the first car race in the United States) with a single cylinder, four horsepower car they had built. Then they sold 13 cars, all the same model, establishing the first auto assembly company in the United States, and the automobile industry was born.

In 1887 Ransom Olds made his first steam-powered car, and then in 1896 he built his first gasoline-powered vehicle. In 1897 he established the Olds Motor Vehicle Company. He was the first car manufacturer to use a stationary assembly line.

The first cars were way too expensive for the average person and appeared to be toys for the rich, so they were not taken very seriously. Then in 1903, a $50 bet began the first road trip across the United States. Horatio Jackson and Sewall Crocker made the trip in 63 days, despite having no useful map, nor paved roads. They followed wagon trails and railroad tracks until they crossed the Mississippi. In Idaho, they acquired a traveling companion, a bulldog named Bud, whom they equipped with goggles to keep the dust out of his eyes. The trip cost Jackson $8000 ($260,000 today) and they never collected on the bet.

After the Henry Ford Motor Company was disbanded and Henry Ford went out on his own, William Murphy and Lemuel Bowen, Ford's financial backers, formed Cadillac Autocar Company which was established on August 22, 1902, and was named after an early French explorer who had founded Detroit in 1701. Cadillac's first cars were the Runabout and the Tonneau, built in 1902. The were 10-horsepower vehicles with a single cylinder engine, and seated two people.

Henry Ford, who had produced a quadricycle in 1896, built his Model T Ford in 1908, at a cost of $850. Then in 1913 he began a moving assembly line, which effectively reduced the cost to $260, making it affordable for the average person.

Since the cranks in the first cars were cumbersome to use, and also dangerous, in 1912 the electric starter was introduced.

I chose the 1896 Duryea for Thaddeus to drive in our story.

Regarding the oil field: At the time of our story, other areas around Butler County were drilling for oil, but El Dorado was not having much success. The two wells they drilled only produced brine, but by 1918, the El

Dorado Oil Field was the largest single field producer in the United States, and was responsible for 12.8% of national oil production and 9% of the world production. It was deemed by some *as the oil field that won World War I.*

ABOUT THE AUTHOR

Best described as a "nice g u y ," Major Mitchell is a former pastor, and credits h i s writing abilities to eight years of writing sermons three times a week. (In truth, he actually began by writing and illustrating comic books as a child). His conversational style immediately engages the reader. He has developed an uncanny eye for detail while c r e a t i n g characters believable enough for the reader to feel that they know them. His ability to create tension will have you turning page after page.

A member of Western Writers of America and a Spur Award finalist for his novel, <u>The Valley of Decision</u>, he has also written several songs, recorded a CD of traditional country/folk music, and occasionally takes the stage as a singer.

Major has 15 novels to his credit, and 3 children's books. He and his wife have recently moved to Idaho where he continues to write and has no inclination to stop.

www.ingramcontent.com/pod-product-compliance
Lightning Source LLC
Chambersburg PA
CBHW050501160726
48003CB00001B/114